CW00666318

"You're Leo N
hot to handle

Leo sighed. "So
Moose for pie and cider?

Fiona shook her head. "Definitely not. The minute I see you in full light, I lose thirty IQ points. Maybe forty."

"And you still won't go out with me?"

"That's right."

Time for a Hail Mary pass. "Then this is it, the last time we'll spend time alone together?"

"Leo, I can't relax and be myself when I'm with you. I wish I could, but—"

"Will you let me kiss you goodbye?"

"What for?"

"To end the evening on a friendly note. I've been thinking about kissing you ever since our date back in August, when it was clear you didn't want that. I've just spent the past three and a half hours thinking about it and hoping this time you would let me kiss you. Give a guy a break."

She hesitated. "I guess that's fair."

Not really. He had no intention of playing fair. Too much was at stake.

SECRET-SANTA COWBOY

THE BUCKSKIN BROTHERHOOD

Vicki Lewis Thompson

Ocean Dance Press

SECRET-SANTA COWBOY
© 2020 Vicki Lewis Thompson

ISBN: 978-1-946759-95-5

Ocean Dance Press LLC
PO Box 69901
Oro Valley, AZ 85737

All Rights Reserved. No part of this book may be used or reproduced or transmitted in any form or by any means, graphic, electronic, or mechanical, including photocopying, recording, taping, or by any information storage or retrieval system, without the written permission of the publisher except in the case of brief quotations embodied in critical articles or reviews.

This is a work of fiction. Any resemblance to actual persons, living or dead, business establishments, events, or locales is entirely coincidental.

Cover art by Lee Hyat Designs

Visit the author's website at
VickiLewisThompson.com

1

Closing at 8 PM for Private Event. The sign hung next to the Choosy Moose entrance. Leo Marston stomped the snow off his boots and breathed in the scent of pine from the wreath on the heavy wooden door.

As Mannheim Steamroller's *Deck the Halls* filtered out to the sidewalk, he glanced at the cowboy standing beside him, his collar turned up against a cold wind. "I look forward to this night all year. You'll love it, Garrett."

"I surely hope so, since nobody's seen fit to tell me what I'm in for."

"Trust me, this is a good surprise." Garrett had hired on at the Buckskin Ranch in April and was still learning the Brotherhood traditions. Leo had the honor of introducing him to this one.

"Whatcha waiting for, Leo?" Jake called out.

He looked over his shoulder at the five guys standing behind them. "Just building the suspense for our first-timer, bro."

"I don't know about Garrett, but I'm on pins and needles. Oh, wait. That's frostbite."

"Okay, okay." Reaching for the brass handle, Leo opened the door with a flourish, waved Garrett inside and stepped in after him.

Garrett stopped dead in his tracks. "Holy moly! Where did all *this* come from?"

"The good people of Apple Grove." Gratitude warmed Leo's chest as he surveyed the bounty. Stepping away from the entry, he made room for the others. "We have our work cut out for us, guys."

"Whoa." Matt thumbed back his hat. "Looks like twice as much as last year."

The white-haired owner of the Choosy Moose, Ben Malone, leaned against the bar. "Folks have been generous."

"They sure have." The sight got to him every time, but tonight's display triggered more throat-clearing than usual. Every table in the place was stacked high with shiny new toys—dolls, trucks, games, trains, stuffed animals, footballs, basketballs, action figures, paints, crayons and blocks. "I hope you picked up extra paper and tape."

"I did. It's on the bandstand."

Garrett's eyes widened. "We're *wrapping* all these?"

"Yessir." Ben straightened and hooked his thumbs in his belt loops. "The townspeople bring in the toys. I donate the hard cider, wrapping supplies and a late-night supper. You boys contribute the labor. Operation Santa is in its tenth year."

"I was here for the first one." Leo shoved his gloves in his coat pocket. "Gets bigger each time, but this...it's way more."

"So many toys." Garrett looked dazed. "I've never seen..."

Leo grinned. Garrett's reaction tickled him. "I can't wait to get started. I'll take your coat and put it on the bar. We generally wear our hats."

"Why?"

"You'll see." He laid both coats in a pile with the others.

"Don't forget to lube up, boys." Ben grabbed a couple of plastic bottles with pump nozzles that had been sitting on the bar. He tossed one toward Leo and the other at CJ.

Leo filled his palm with lotion before passing the bottle to Garrett. "Thanks for remembering, Ben. Whoever found that tip online—"

"That would be me." Jake took the bottle from CJ, squirted out a liberal amount and gave the bottle to Rafe. "Always looking out for you guys."

Garrett sniffed the nozzle and handed the bottle to Matt. "I'll pass."

Matt handed it back. "Better take some, buddy."

"Why? It smells flowery. I don't want to—"

"Paper cuts. The lotion protects your hands."

Garrett snorted. "Paper cuts? I'm not worried about—"

"You will be if you don't put this on, big guy." CJ worked the lotion into his hands. "Before Jake found this hack, I'd have bloody guitar strings for at least a week afterward."

Garrett shrugged and took the bottle from Matt. "Then I guess I'll smell like a rose garden."

"They had the unscented kind," Ben said. "But this was cheaper and contrary to what you might think, it doesn't subtract from your manliness. In fact, Henri likes the smell when I put it on my hands. Or on—"

"Hold up, there, Ben." Jake gave him a warning glance. "I'm cool with you dating our boss lady, but I don't want details."

"I put lotion on my *face,* son. I'm not about to tell you what else I do with it."

"Good. Let's change the subject. I saw a video online with a new technique for wrapping odd-shaped objects. I'll be happy to share."

"About time." Leo crossed to a table and picked up a football. "My wrapped balls still look like a five-year-old did it." He sent the football spiraling toward Nick.

Nick caught it one-handed and threw it to Jake. "Balls are tough to wrap."

Jake laughed and tossed the ball to Matt. "I could say something."

"Don't," Matt said. "Let's keep it clean a little longer. We have a newbie." He let go with a rainbow pass to Rafe, who'd wandered over to the bandstand to inspect the rolls of Christmas wrap.

"I'm for that." Rafe caught it effortlessly before firing it toward CJ, who completed the round by tossing it to Garrett.

"Are we graded on our wrapping job?" Garrett spun the ball in his hands. "Because I can't wrap worth a damn. I require about fifty feet of tape for each package."

"We're persnickety at the beginning," Jake said, "but after a few rounds of cider, we loosen up."

Ben rolled his eyes. "Yeah, you do." He looked over at Garrett. "Last year they decided to wrap Merlin." He gestured to the life-sized plush moose head mounted over the bar. "It didn't go well."

"It would have been easier if we could have taken him down," Rafe said. "It's tough to wrap something when you're standing on the bar."

"Merlin stays put." Ben swept a glance around the room. "And he does not get wrapped."

Rafe nodded. "Understood. Can we stick bows on him, though?"

"If you must."

"We must," Rafe said. "Garrett, since you ended up with the football, you get to choose a toy category."

Garrett glanced around the room. "Board games."

Matt groaned. "I knew it. Easiest—"

"Action figures!" CJ and Nick called out together, followed quickly by Jake shouting *blocks* at the same time Rafe did.

The haggling over categories continued as two tables were cleared and pushed together to create a workspace. Ben served everybody hard cider dressed in knit holiday bottle huggers to control bottle sweat.

Leo went behind the bar and turned up the music. When he'd signed on at the Buckskin he'd told anybody who'd listen that he'd lost the Christmas spirit. Operation Santa had given it back to him.

* * *

Two hours later, Merlin was covered with stick-on bows and every cowboy had at least one bow on his hat. The tables were bare and brightly wrapped packages filled the entire bandstand. Each bore a coded tag with a child's first and last name.

Rafe manned a broom, sweeping up the last bits of wrapping paper and any hopelessly crushed bows. The rich aroma of barbequed pork drifted from the kitchen where Jake and Ben were making hot sandwiches and country fries.

Leo added his last package to the pile and returned to his chair. "We did it."

"Yeah, we did." Nick pulled his bottle hugger off his empty one, went behind the bar and tugged it on a fresh brew. He glanced up at the moose head. "Merlin looks good, but I still think Ben should have let us wrap his antlers. We were responsible this time. We put down rags before we stood on the bar."

"Maybe next year." Matt sipped his coffee. He and Leo were the designated drivers, so they'd switched from cider to coffee midway through.

"Wrapping makes you hungry." Garrett had stuck a bow to the front of his shirt in addition to the one on his hat. He didn't tend to get toasted at Brotherhood events, but he sounded like he had a buzz going tonight. "I never knew that."

"Food's up!" Jake called from the kitchen. "Come dish yourselves."

Leo followed Garrett in. "Have fun?"

"Big fun." He glanced over his shoulder. "Overdid the cider, though. Glad you're driving back."

"Happy to. It's your first toy-wrapping. I wanted you to relax and get into it."

"I surely did. It's great to know those kids will have something to open on Christmas morning. Wish I could see their faces."

"You will. We get pictures."

"We do?"

"The parents always send them to Ben, who forwards them to Ed. She makes a quick video with a Christmas music soundtrack and emails the link to Henri. We usually watch that before Christmas dinner."

"Very cool."

Garrett didn't know the half of it. Leo had spent ten memorable Christmas seasons at the Buckskin.

The ranch was closed to guests for two weeks, giving Henri and the staff much-needed down time. Except for caring for the horses, which Leo enjoyed, the Brotherhood had no official duties. The holiday had gone from his least favorite to his most cherished one of all.

After loading their plates with barbeque sandwiches and chunky country fries, the men grabbed their spot around the former wrapping station and tucked into the dinner. Conversation halted for a while.

Garrett was the first one finished with his meal. He tucked his napkin under his plate and leaned back in his chair. "How do you distribute the toys?"

"That's Ben's job," Matt said. "He puts on the Santa suit tomorrow night, hops in his red truck and delivers a sack to each family." He glanced around the table. "We still have to put the toys in the sacks, by the way."

"It won't take long," Ben said. "Now that we've coded the tags, it's easy."

Garrett looked confused. "But tomorrow is only the twenty-first. Why not Christmas Eve?"

"I thought about doing that. But lots of folks attend Christmas Eve services, including families where I'd be making deliveries. Half the fun is letting the kids see Santa. I picked the twenty-first because it's Yule, the winter solstice."

"Don't they wonder why Santa's a few days ahead of schedule?"

"I tell them the special kids receive their gifts on Yule. It's nice, in a way, because many of them worry they won't get anything come the twenty-fifth. This way they know they'll have something to open on the big day."

"Do they wait for it?"

"Sure do, because Santa tells them that's how it's done."

Garrett smiled. "Nice. Big job, though."

"I always take a helper. They wear an elf suit. Used to be my wife Suzanne until she passed, but after that I started choosing someone who was new in town." Ben glanced at Garrett. "But before you ask, it's not you. Maybe next year, if you're up to wearing an elf costume."

"If I can rub rose-scented lotion on my hands, guess I could wear an elf costume."

"Is it Henri?" Rafe pushed aside his empty plate. "Some of us thought you might ask her to go, since—"

"We talked about it, but she likes the current tradition. It's a great way for a new person to find out what Apple Grove is all about."

Rafe nodded. "Kate loved doing it her first year in town."

"I'll bet Isabel would have, too," CJ said, "but I can see why you wouldn't ask a woman who could go into labor at any minute."

Ben laughed. "Yep. A little too Biblical for me."

"So who is it?" By process of elimination, Leo had a pretty good idea.

"I decided to go with someone who's been here a few months longer than Garrett—Fiona Hildebrand."

Yep. "She'll love it." His quick response was a defense against the stab of regret every time Fiona was mentioned. He was happy for her, though. She'd have a ball.

But his rapid-fire comment had drawn attention and his brothers were sneaking glances his way. Ben likely wasn't aware that Fiona was a sore point with him.

At the bachelor auction in August, she'd outbid everyone to win the dinner date he'd offered. Then she'd barely talked to him all evening. Confused, he'd asked her out again and she'd put him on hold. Permanently, it seemed.

He didn't get it. And he still had no answers even though she was one of Eva Kilpatrick's best friends and Nick was now living with Eva. Nick had to know more than he was telling.

Jake, always good about diffusing awkward situations, brought up the weather forecast for the following night. Snow was predicted. Because that was often the case, the reusable toy bags were weatherproof.

When the meal was over, the guys bagged the toys and the party broke up. CJ, Rafe and Jake climbed into Matt's truck. Leo took Garrett and Nick. Nick sat in the back seat because he'd be dropped off first at Eva's house a few blocks away.

Leo glanced over his shoulder as he pulled away from the Moose. "Look, bro, I have to believe Eva knows why Fiona won't date me. Which means logically that you know, too. I'd consider it a kindness if you'd level with me."

Nick sighed. "Even if it's something you can't fix?"

"Yes, damn it!" He met Nick's gaze in the rearview mirror. "I just need to know."

"You're too handsome."

"What the hell?"

"It sounds ridiculous, especially to those of us who know you, but Fiona's kind of a geeky girl and..."

"I *like* that about her! She started talking about Pluto and why it should be labeled a planet. Then she abruptly ended the discussion."

"She figured you wouldn't want to talk about Pluto."

"Why not?"

"Because you don't look like a geek."

"Oh, for God's sake."

"Hey, you asked and I'm only reporting what I've heard from Eva. Bidding on you was a big step out of Fiona's comfort zone. She was so dazzled by your star power that she couldn't relax."

"She didn't seem that tense when I drove her home the night of the auction."

"I asked Eva about that. Fiona was tired after a long day and she'd had two or three glasses of champagne at Ed's party. That mellowed her out. Since your date was Sunday night, she had all day to obsess. And she was afraid to order alcohol for fear she'd make a fool of herself."

"I wondered why she passed on having a drink since she'd seemed to enjoy the champagne."

"Face it, bro. That mug of yours is as perfect as any of those guys making millions in blockbuster movies. She can't handle it."

"That sucks."

"Which is why I haven't brought it up. It's not like you can do anything about how you look."

"Except wear a bag over your head." Garrett laughed. "Wait, that wouldn't work. She'd recognize your manly body. You'd have to wear something to disguise all of you."

The solution hit him fully formed, ready to be deployed. "Like a Santa suit?"

<u>2</u>

"You won't be Santa this year?" Fiona didn't care for this shift in plans, but she couldn't back out at the last minute. The toy delivery was due to start in two hours. At least Ben had come over to her shop to give her the news in person. "What about the kids you visited last year? Won't they notice it's not the same Santa?"

"I doubt it. Clark's about my size, and he has a deep voice. He's a pretty good mimic so he can probably sound exactly like me if he puts his mind to it."

"That would be helpful."

"Besides, he'll have on the suit, the beard, and the padding around his waist. The kids who've been through this before will assume it's me, or rather, Santa, depending on how young they are."

"Does he know the routine? The route?"

"I've given him all the info he'll need. He'll pick you up in front of the shop at six on the dot. It's on his bucket list to play Santa and pass out toys to needy children. He loves Christmas and this means a lot to him."

"What's his last name?"

"Smith."

"I don't remember meeting anyone named Clark Smith."

"Well, he's—"

"I've only been here a little over a year, though. It's not like I know everybody."

"You'll like him. He and my wife Suzanne were good friends."

"An older gentleman, then?" She flushed. "Not that you're old, Ben. I didn't mean—"

"I'm old enough to be your father, so that puts me in senior citizen territory. But Clark's around your age."

"Huh. What does he do?"

"Works with horses."

"A cowboy?"

"You could call him that. Hey, does the elf outfit fit okay?"

"It does. I'm glad it's roomy enough for me to put on thermal underwear. I tried on everything last night and went outside. I wasn't that cold."

"You can wear a coat except when you get out to help Santa."

"Oh, I will. But the snow they predicted is moving off to the north. I was kind of disappointed. Delivering toys while it's snowing would add to the atmosphere."

"I'd rather you had a safe trip than atmosphere."

"Good point. Don't want Santa stuck in a snowdrift."

"For sure. Listen, I need to take off and gas up the red truck, but I want to buy Henri a journal while I'm here. She's been talking about starting one, now that she's about to be a grandma. I thought it might make a good Christmas present."

"Great idea. Let's look at what I have." She walked over to a shelf dedicated to nothing but journals. They were arranged spines out because she had a large selection.

"She'll want it to have recycled paper."

"That's all I carry."

"So that's why you call the place *Planet-Friendly Paper*. I wondered." He scanned the array and pulled out a leather-covered journal. "This looks like something Henri would like. What about leather? Is that recycled, too?"

"Absolutely. The company that makes those uses discarded leather items like coats, chaps, boots..."

"Henri will approve of that concept, too." He opened the journal and leafed through the pages. "The paper has an antique look. Classy. I'll take it."

"Do you need it gift-wrapped?"

"No, ma'am. I'll handle that. But you know what? I should warn you that I bought regular Christmas wrap and stick-on bows for Operation Santa."

"No worries. I understand." She smiled. "I'm guessing the families preserve the paper and reuse the bows."

"That's what I hear."

She stepped behind the counter and rang up the purchase. "Any word on how soon Isabel and CJ can expect that baby girl?"

"The doc says any day, but then again, maybe not until after the first of the year. Henri's so excited she can't stand it. I may give this to her tonight instead of waiting. She can pour some of her excess energy into writing love notes to little Cleo Marie." He handed her cash.

"Do you need a receipt?"

"No, ma'am, don't need that, either."

She counted out his change. 'The paper's acid-free, so it will last a while."

"That's great. She plans to give the journal to Cleo when she's old enough to read cursive."

"Aww. What a sweet project. Does she need pens?"

"I'll check. If she does, I'll be back." Touching two fingers to the brim of his Stetson, he started for the door just as Beth came through it. "Hey, there! How're things at Racy Lace?"

"Busy! 'Tis the season to be sexy." She unbuttoned her coat. "I keep expecting you to come in and buy something seductive for Henri."

He laughed. "That's funny. The boys don't want to hear a word about our sex life and here you are encouraging me to spice it up."

"Because I don't think of her as my mom. Seriously, you should come by. I have something I know she'd love."

"I promise I'll be in. Gotta run—truck needs gas."

"Have fun tonight."

"I won't—on second thought, I'll let Fiona tell you about that. See you ladies later." Tipping his hat, he hurried out the door.

Beth walked toward the register. "Tell me what?"

"He gave the Santa job to someone named Clark Smith."

"He's not doing it? That's disappointing. I wanted you to have the same experience I had last year."

"Me, too."

"Who's Clark Smith?"

"No clue. Never heard of the guy. Evidently he desperately wants to take this on and Ben says I'll like him. I'm a little bummed about it, but what can I do? Ben's in charge of this venture, so if he wants to give his spot to someone else, that's his privilege."

"I saw he bought a journal."

"For Henri. She wants to record this first grandma experience."

"It's a thoughtful gift, but I'm pretty sure she's also expecting saucy nightwear."

"Nightwear he can't let the Brotherhood know he purchased. What a riot. Those guys are doing the deed with their chosen sweethearts, but they don't want to think of Henri having a good time."

"I know. But she's the mom figure. I get it."

"And the grandma figure. CJ and Isabel will be tickled that she's journaling about their kid. Which reminds me, I finished reading the risqué diary Eva found in her attic this summer."

"Stimulating reading, isn't it?"

"No kidding. Miss Barton and her secret lover certainly enjoyed themselves in that Victorian."

"Have you had time to look through the *Gazette* archives to see if you can figure out who he was?"

"Got a start on it. I have some likely candidates. I'd love to solve the mystery, especially if he's still around."

"But you wouldn't unmask him."

"God, no. That wouldn't be right. I'll just tell you and Eva. So what are you up to tonight?"

"I'm spending the night out at Jared's. We're building a fire and watching Christmas movies."

"I'll bet you *build a fire.*" She made air quotes.

Beth laughed. "We literally build a fire. That's not to say we don't get frisky on the couch while we're watching the movie."

"You could just stay out there, you know. He has to come in to Logan's Leathers every day and you could ride in with him and then go back every evening."

"It's been discussed. But I love my little apartment over the shop. I love Jared, too, and I'm thrilled that we got past our misunderstandings, but...I don't want to give up—" She threw her hands in the air. "It's hard to explain."

"I see what you mean, though. Your shops are connected. Living at his ranch would mean being accessible to each other twenty-four-seven. No matter how much you love each other, that's a lot of together time."

"And maybe someday I'll want that. Not yet."

"Then listen to your gut."

"Aren't you supposed to listen to your heart?"

"Hell, no. Your heart will screw you up every time. Your gut tells the truth."

"Wise words." Beth came over and gave her a hug. "Good luck with Clark Smith." She paused. "Does that sound like an alias to you?"

"The Smith part does, but not Clark. Joe Smith or Bill Smith would have been suspicious. Not Clark."

"Clark Kent would have been suspicious."

Fiona laughed. "You think? Or Clark Griswold. Even *more* suspicious, since we're doing a Christmas thing. But Clark Smith is just some nice guy who wants the Santa experience."

"Do you know anything about him?

"Ben said he works with horses, so I'm picturing a cowboy. I'm sure he'll be fine."

"Can't wait to hear about it tomorrow." She buttoned her coat.

"Bottom line, some kids who wouldn't get much for Christmas will have toys to play with on Christmas Day."

"That's the important thing." Beth turned as the shop door jingled. "You have customers. See you in the morning!" She skirted around the group of teenage girls who came in and slipped outside.

The girls needed art supplies for a school project they'd be working on during the Christmas break. They were in high spirits as they looked forward to two weeks with no classes and their bouncy mood carried Fiona through to five o'clock.

After closing out the register and straightening the displays, she quickly vacuumed the floor before hurrying up to her apartment. Dinner was a PB&J sandwich and a cup of tea. Then she stripped down, tugged on her thermal underwear and put on the fleece elf suit that Beth had worn a year earlier.

Green pants cuffed in red were paired with a red tunic. Its green collar and cuffs matched the pants and the saw-tooth hem gave it an elfin look. Red elf boots, more like slipper socks than shoes, had turned-up toes and a little bell. A red and green fleece stocking cap completed the outfit.

She left her hair loose and pulled the stocking cap over her ears. Beth had worn the cap on the back of her head and glued on pointy ears, but she'd skipped that embellishment.

Yikes, almost six. Grabbing her wool coat and gloves, which luckily were a matching red, she hurried to the front window and peered out.

The guy was early. Ben's red truck, the back mounded with bags of toys, was diagonally parked in front of her shop with the engine running. Clouds of condensed moisture poured from the tailpipe.

What was his name again? Chuck Smith? No, Clark. Clark Smith. Did she need her purse? No, it would just get in the way. Snatching her key from a hook by the stairs, she tucked it in her coat pocket, picked up her phone and made for the stairs. The map function on her phone might come in handy.

Whoa, better not take the stairs fast in elf boots. Tumbling to the bottom wouldn't help the situation. She descended carefully.

When she walked out the door, Santa climbed down from the truck. Terrific suit. Looked like red velvet trimmed with faux ermine.

His belt was black and shiny with a big brass buckle. His black boots were shiny, too. Even his beard looked real.

He wore wire-rimmed glasses, which might be his, but if they were, they fit the costume perfectly. He had on gloves instead of mittens, but that was the only departure from tradition. Made sense from a dexterity standpoint.

"Fabulous outfit, Santa."

"Thanks, Fiona. Is it okay if I call you that?"

"As opposed to what?"

"Miss Hildebrand."

"Good grief. Please call me Fiona, or Fi."

"Alrighty, then, Fi. I'm Clark." He took off his glove and held out his hand. "And thanks for putting up with the change in plans."

She peered at him as they shook hands. Light reflected off his glasses and she couldn't see his eyes very well. "You do sound like Ben. He said you were a good mimic."

"Did some acting when I was younger. I'm glad you brought a coat, but you won't need it in the truck. I've turned up the heat."

"Then let's go." She started toward the passenger side. "I bought super good thermal underwear when I decided to move to Montana. And my costume is polyester, so it's warm."

"So is mine, and I have padding. I might have to turn the heat down before the night's over." He opened the passenger door and warm air spilled out. "Yeah, might need to do it now."

She accepted his help getting in. "I appreciate the hand up. These elf shoes will take some getting used to. I almost fell down the stairs."

"Then please watch your step." He closed the door and rounded the truck. When he got behind the wheel, he glanced at her. "Too hot?"

"It's pretty warm."

"Then let's back it off a bit." He adjusted the heater before pulling the door closed. "That should be better."

"Wow, I would swear that was Ben talking just now."

"I practiced some today, getting into character. I asked him to record his voice for me and that helped a lot."

"You're taking this seriously, aren't you?"

"Absolutely. He's doing me a big favor by letting me impersonate him this year. Don't want to screw it up."

"I wouldn't worry about that. Clearly you're a detail-oriented person. You'll be fine."

"Nice of you to say. Want some music?"

"Seems like we should have music, right? I brought my phone."

"So did I." He picked it up from the cup holder. "Got any favorites?"

"Anything by Mannheim Steamroller works for me."

"Good, we agree." He tapped on the screen and *Deck the Halls* flowed from the truck's speakers.

"Well done! This isn't even your truck and you synced your phone to the speakers. I'm impressed."

He grinned. "Ben insists it doesn't have that function. I figured it must have since it's only two years old and its loaded with options, so I drove over here early and set it up while I waited for you."

"Which means if I had done this with Ben instead of you, the music option would have been…"

"Holiday tunes on the radio."

"I prefer this option."

"Me, too." He turned on the dome light and popped open the console. "Here's our list of deliveries." He handed it to her. "The one at the top, the Emerson place, is the farthest away. I know where that one is, but after that, I'll need some guidance as we work our way back."

"Aha! Exactly why I brought this." She held up her phone.

"Excellent. You're in charge of navigation."

"I assume the bags are labeled."

"Yep, and the last delivery was loaded first. Ready to deliver toys to excited kids?"

"I sure am."

"Let's do it." He shut off the dome light and backed out of the parking space as the tune switched to *We Three Kings*. "Ben said he always takes a turn around the square before heading out. Sets the mood."

"Good idea." She gazed out the window as he slowly drove past storefronts dressed for the season, streetlamps decorated with wreaths and red bows, and the jewel in the middle—a gazebo festooned with greenery, bows and a glittering Christmas tree in the center.

She had a view of the square from her shop and her apartment, but it sparkled a little brighter tonight. Her disappointment at not having the Ben Malone experience had vanished. Instead she'd have the Clark Smith experience, and it was shaping up to be just as good and maybe a teensy bit better.

3

Like night and day. Leo couldn't get over the difference between this Fiona and the nervous, mostly silent woman he'd taken to dinner at the Moose four months ago. Evidently a disguise changed everything.

Bottom line, he had one evening to convince her the man behind the face was someone she might like to know. As he left the square, he turned the music down slightly. "How much did Ben tell you about how this goes?"

"Not much, but my friend Beth—do you know Beth?"

"I know who she is."

"She was Santa's elf last year. She had a blast. She was excited that I'd get to do it. I'm wearing the same outfit she did."

"Looks good on you." Adorable, in fact, but saying that would sound weird at this point.

"Thanks. The pants are a little short, but since the boots come up past my ankles, it doesn't matter. The kids will be paying more attention to you, anyway."

"Maybe, although those pointy shoes with a jingle bell look like crowd pleasers to me."

"They're stylin', all right." She raised one foot and wiggled it so the bell would ring. "They're my favorite part of the costume."

"I can see why. By the way, Ben reminded me to greet the kids by name if possible. Their ages are on the list so that should help me identify who's who. If you'll prompt me with that info as we pull up, that'll help enormously."

"You bet."

"Ben treats his helper to pumpkin pie and warm cider at the Moose afterward, but he'll be out at Henri's when we get back. Would you let me buy you dessert when we get back?"

"Sounds lovely. I accept."

It was all so easy, now that he was in disguise. The woman who had put him off indefinitely when he'd asked for a second date had immediately agreed to a nightcap. "Doesn't have to be pie and cider."

"Oh, yes, it does. Beth told me that finished off the evening perfectly."

"Alrighty, then. What else did she say? I don't want to leave out anything significant."

"She mentioned they drove through a light snow, which made the night even more magical, but that's pretty much out of your control."

"You never know. I'm Santa Claus. I'll work on it. What else?"

"Ben, I mean *Santa*, gave her some history on the apple orchards Orville Dubois planted and his decision to name the town Apple Grove, but I've researched Orville on my own, so that part isn't necessary."

"That's a relief. I know some of that, but I've never heard Orville's last name. To me, he's just Orville, the nice old guy who hangs out by the pot-bellied stove at the Apple Barrel and can tell you more about growing apples than anybody in Montana. Is he French?"

"His parents were French immigrants, so he can probably speak the language. He married a local schoolteacher but she died young. He never remarried, so I think she was the love of his life."

"Where did you learn all this?"

"Back issues of the *Gazette*. Small-town papers are great fun to read."

"They have the actual newspapers tucked away somewhere?"

"No, those would be crumbling to dust by now, but a forward-thinking person digitized them before that happened."

"Are you a history buff?"

"Not all history, but this little town and its inhabitants fascinate me. When I get hooked on something, I like to dig into every aspect of it. One day I'd like to sit down with Henri Fox and hear more about the history of her ranch."

"I'm sure she'd enjoy that."

"You know Henri?"

Uh-oh. "Doesn't everybody?"

"I suppose that's true. And clearly you know Ben, so logically you know Henri. Ben mentioned you wanted this gig because you're a big fan of Christmas."

"I am."

"What's your favorite part?"

"I like all of it, but I have a feeling tonight might turn out to be my favorite. What's yours?"

"Good question."

"Mannheim Steamroller?"

"Probably, now that you mention it. I like the spin they put on the traditional carols."

"How about Christmas trees? Everybody usually likes—"

"The one on the square is beautiful. Personally, I've never had one."

"Are you opposed to cutting them?"

"Not if they're harvested responsibly. But I'm not steeped in the usual traditions like so many people. My parents have never celebrated Christmas. They say it's too commercial."

Her stance surprised the heck out of him. "It certainly can be." Before signing on at the Buckskin, he would have agreed with her folks. "Does Ben know this about you?"

"He might. I haven't made a secret of it. I decorated the store for the holidays because that makes good business sense. I play Christmas music in the store and wish everyone a Merry Christmas, but I haven't been moved to get a tree for my apartment."

"Why did you agree to be Santa's elf?"

"Are you kidding? That's a huge honor and I'll be helping pass out toys to kids who don't have much. Beth couldn't say enough about what fun she had. I wasn't going to turn down the chance just because I'm not totally into Christmas."

He got it, now. Ben might have had other candidates for the job, like Garrett, for instance. But for a Christmas cheerleader like Ben, the chance to make a convert had been irresistible. Then he'd entrusted the job to Leo.

No worries. He could do two things at once. He was Santa. He had powers. And questions. "If your folks don't approve of Christmas, how do they avoid it? It's everywhere."

"They suffer through November and half of December. Then they take off for some remote area for two or three weeks. They told me where they were going this year but I honestly can't remember. I just know they'll be out of cellphone range most of the time."

"Did they invite you to go along?"

She laughed. "Naturally, but this is my busiest time, my most lucrative couple of weeks. Ironic, huh?"

"Do you think the merchants in Apple Grove commercialize Christmas?"

"Not really. Do they take advantage of the gift-giving season? Sure. That's good business. I do it, too. But it's not hard-sell, in your face."

"And it doesn't start too early."

"That's huge. It became obvious when I was location scouting. I came to town the second week in November. Not a hint of Christmas anywhere. I asked around and learned that nothing Christmas-related happens until after Thanksgiving weekend."

"Is that why you chose this town?"

"One of the reasons. I was also determined to get out of my comfort zone by choosing somewhere totally different from where I grew up."

"Where was that?"

"Phoenix. Tempe, more precisely. My folks are college professors at ASU. I was supposed to be one, too. They think I've lost my mind."

"Mine think the same about me."

"Oh, yeah? What were you supposed to be?"

"Famous."

"Doing what?"

"I need to take a rain check on that topic." Thank God. He could kick himself for saying as much as he had. Way to blow his cover too early. "We're almost to the Emerson place. What are the kids' names? I remember Bobbie. Is the next one Jackie?"

"Let me look. Yes. Bobbie is seven and Jackie is five. Molly is twenty months."

"Bobbie, then Jackie, then Molly. Got it." He turned off the main road where a battered mailbox was lettered with the name *Emerson.* He'd been out here a couple of years ago, before Molly was born. The Babes had heard that Bob Emerson was laid up with a bum ankle, his wife was pregnant, and they had a major fence issue that needed attention.

The Brotherhood had fixed the fence and rounded up the sheep that had escaped. Trudy Emerson had insisted on making them lunch. They'd eaten sparingly, but refusing what she'd offered would have been rude.

Bob and Trudy worked hard and cared deeply for each other. Thank goodness they'd reached out to Ben for help with Christmas gifts for the kids.

Although there wasn't much of a yard, they'd created a walkway of salvaged bricks that led up to the front porch. A string of Christmas lights stretched across the eaves. A tree placed in a front window glowed with lights, too. Bob and Trudy were doing their best.

Leo pulled up next to the walkway and the porch light flicked on. "I'd like to help you down, Fi, but I think it's best if we exit fast and meet by the tailgate."

"Right on, Santa. Bobbie, Jackie and Molly."

"Thanks." He shut off the motor, climbed out as quickly as the bulky suit allowed, and hurried to the back of the truck.

Fiona, dressed in a more forgiving outfit than his, beat him there. She grabbed the tailgate and lowered it with brisk efficiency. "Which bag?"

"One of these on the top layer, and it's marked, but it's black as pitch back here. I should've—"

"Allow me, Santa." Fiona activated her flashlight on her phone and scanned the tags. "This one."

He grabbed it off the top of the pile and slung it over his shoulder. "Have you done this before?"

"No, but I'm a quick study."

"Just how smart are you?"

"Let's just say that nobody could beat me at Tetris. This bag arrangement reminds me of it."

"I wonder if I have that app on my phone."

"Not now. The Emersons just came out the front door. It's show time."

4

The Emerson kids were on springs, hopping around the porch in giddy abandon. Fiona wanted to run up the steps and dance with those cuties. All three were curly-haired redheads like their mom. They wore jackets over their pajamas but only Molly's was zipped. Their parents tried in vain to settle them down.

Clark approached the porch with a hearty *ho, ho, ho*, and a jolly *Merry Christmas.* The closer he got, the quieter Molly became. The other two stopped jumping, too, gazing at Santa with rapt attention as he lowered his sack to the porch steps. Molly scooted behind her mom's leg and peered out at the large man in the red and white suit.

Crouching, Clark put himself at eye level with her. "Hello, Molly." His gentle tone mimicked Ben's exactly.

She ducked behind her mom, poked her head out once, eyes wide, and hastily retreated again.

"She's shy." Jackie hopped down one step. "I'm not. I'm *five.*" She held up one hand, fingers spread.

Clark held up his gloved hand, palm out. "Congrats, Jackie."

She smacked her palm against his and grinned. "Thanks." She jumped down another step. "Who's that?" She pointed toward Fiona.

"Sorry, I should have introduced her first thing. I'd like you all to meet...Perky, my number one elf." He glanced her way and winked.

Perky? He'd clearly come up with that on the fly. She could do better. By the next stop, she'd have a new name. She smiled and sketched a bow. "Pleased to meet all of you."

Jackie swung her arms back and forth. "Where's your reindeer?"

"I gave them time off."

"Oh. That's nice. Aren't you gonna ask me if I've been good?"

Clark choked and cleared his throat. "I was just getting to that."

"I've been good *all* the time. Except for breaking a glass on accident. I don't get in trouble like *Bobbie.* He—"

"I don't get in trouble *that* much." He walked down two steps and stuck out his hand. "Pleased to meet you, Mr. Claus."

Fiona melted. Such a grown-up boy. Jackie was a kick and Molly...oh, my God...too cute for words. She wanted to take them all home.

"Pleased to meet you, Bobbie." Clark shook his hand. Then he rose to his feet. "Well, Perky, we have Jackie, who's always good and Bobbie, who's usually good, and Molly, who we'll assume is good, so—"

"Not *always*." Jackie looked over her shoulder at her little sister. "She pulls hair."

Bobbie sighed. "She does, but she's getting better. She should get presents, too."

Molly popped out from behind her mother's thigh. "Me, too!" She giggled and disappeared again.

Clark turned his laughter into a cough. Then he cleared his throat. "Perky, would you like to help me pass out their gifts?"

"I sure would, Santa!" Maybe Clark couldn't let himself laugh. Mimicking Ben's voice was doable. Mimicking his laugh, or anyone's for that matter, would be tricky.

"One more thing, kids." He turned and gazed solemnly at Bobbie and Jackie. "Promise me you'll wait and open your presents on Christmas."

Bobbie snapped to attention. "Yes, sir."

Jackie considered the matter for a couple of seconds. Then she nodded. "Okay, I promise, but Mommy and Daddy have to watch Molly. She won't wait."

"We'll watch her, punkin," her dad said. "We'll put her presents in a safe place."

After Clark opened the bag, Fiona helped him sort through the contents—nine gifts, three for each child. Fiona quietly handed Molly's up to her mother, but gave the two older kids theirs to hold.

Bobbie cradled his carefully and said *thank you* each time one was handed to him.

Jackie did some squeezing and shaking of hers before looking up at Clark. "I was just *feeling* them. I won't open a *single one.*"

He smiled. "I'm counting on you."

"You can, Santa. You really can." Her eyes glowed with excitement.

Bobbie's face lit up, too, although he was working hard to keep his cool.

Molly came out from behind her mother, dropped to her hands and knees and started crawling backwards down the steps, clearly ready to get in on whatever was happening. "Me, too! Me, too!"

Her dad retrieved her, which didn't go well. She wiggled and protested. "Down! Down!"

Fiona glanced at Clark. "What now?"

"I've got this." Digging to the bottom of the sack, he came up with a plush moose the size of his fist. "There's two more in there." He climbed the steps and held out the moose. "Here you go, Molly."

Fiona located the other two and passed them to Bobbie and Jackie. Then she glanced at Molly, who'd clutched the soft toy to her chest and started crooning to it. Disaster averted.

The little girl looked up, smiled at Clark and angled her body in his direction, lips puckered.

Her dad laughed. "She wants to give you a kiss. She's learned that's a good way to thank people."

"I'd be honored." Clark leaned in, offering his cheek.

She pressed her rosebud mouth to it. Then she giggled and made a grab for his beard.

He dodged, but she managed to tangle her fingers in the fake hair. The beard started to give way.

"Hey, kids!" Fiona made a quick bid for their attention. "Want to see me dance a jig?" Arms propped at her hips, she did her best imitation of the Irish step dancers she's seen in concert several times. She made those little bells tinkle like crazy.

Her efforts weren't professional quality, but they entertained Bobbie and Jackie long enough for the two parents to loosen Molly's grip and for Clark to adjust his beard.

During that process, Fiona got a glimpse of a square, smooth-shaven jaw. If the rest of his face matched that manly jaw....

Was Clark nice-looking under the beard, mustache and fake eyebrows? Ben had said he was about her age. Was he single? Likely he was if he'd chosen to deliver presents instead of snuggling with his sweetheart tonight.

His strong desire to play Santa for little kids was appealing and he seemed to be having fun doing it. Ben liked and trusted him or he wouldn't have handed over the job.

The possibility that Clark might be...well, a *possibility* intrigued her. So far she'd enjoyed herself. He was easy to talk to and evidently they shared a similar background—taking a career path totally different from the one their respective parents had envisioned.

Once the beard was firmly in place, Clark turned to her. "Time to make our next delivery, Perky!

"Aye, aye, Santa! Merry Christmas, everybody!" She blew them all kisses as she grabbed the empty bag and hurried back to the truck.

Clark said his goodbyes, waved and caught up with her in time to hand her into the truck. "Just toss the empty bag in the back seat."

"Got it. She fastened her seat belt and grabbed her phone to key in the next address.

Rounding the hood, he opened the driver's door, stood on the running board and raised his voice. "Merry Christmas to all, and to all a good night!" Then he slid into the seat, closed the door and buckled up. "We need to make tracks." He backed around and headed down the dirt road.

"Yeah, we do." She counted the names on the list. "If we take that much time with each family, we'll be done around—"

"Three in the morning?"

She laughed. "Something like that. I have the next place located. Left at the main road, right at the four-way stop, third house on the right."

"Great. Thanks. How many kids?"

"Only one. Georgie Warner. Single mom. Shouldn't take as long."

"I sure lost track of time at the Emerson place. That Jackie is something else."

"She's a pip, all right. Total contrast to her adorably proper brother."

"And Molly! What a cutie-pie. Ben warned me it would be a challenge to keep things moving. I assured him I'd have no trouble getting it all done by nine."

"Nine?"

"If we don't, the kids will be in bed. Nine's the outer limit."

"Good point." She counted the names on the list. "We're in trouble."

"I know. Nice dance, by the way."

"I don't think Jackie and Bobbie saw anything."

"I know Jackie didn't. She's such a pistol she would have asked how come my beard wasn't attached."

Fiona laughed. "That's for sure."

"I should've anticipated Molly would make that move. Jackie warned me her sister pulls hair. How old is Georgie?"

"Two and a half."

"He might be past the hair-pulling stage, but I won't take any chances."

"Would you like me to keep track of the time for you?"

"That would be awesome. How about a reminder at the five-minute mark?"

"Sure. I'll glance at my phone and say *Incoming message from Mrs. Claus.*"

"Perfect. Gives me a graceful way to speed things up. Okay, third house, you said?"

"Yep. The yellow one with the porch light on."

"I couldn't do this without you, Perky."

"We're changing my name, by the way."

"You don't like Perky?"

"Nope. I prefer Galadriel."

"From Lord of the Rings?"

"Yessir."

He laughed. "I like it. Suits your blond hair, too. Galadriel it is."

"Are you a fan?" His laugh was familiar. Where had she heard it before?

"I've only seen the movies. Never read the books. My little sis, though, she's read them all, more than once. She owns the movies, too."

"So do I. And the books. Does your sister live in Apple Grove? We could geek out together over Tolkien."

"Penelope doesn't live here. Wish she did." He pulled to a stop in front of the yellow house. "I saw a little face peeking out the window. We'd better get a move on."

"Yep." She flipped open her seat belt. They couldn't afford to dawdle, but she wished they hadn't had to interrupt the conversation just when it was getting interesting.

She wanted to know more about his Tolkien-obsessed sister. And why his parents had expected him to become famous.

Oh, and next time they had a chance to talk, she'd think of a joke. Maybe a Christmas joke. She wanted to hear him laugh again. Maybe that would jog her memory about where she'd heard it.

5

Leo swiftly left the truck, both to speed up the delivery of toys and slow down his delivery of personal info. Giving Fiona a chance to know and like him without revealing his identity was a complicated dance.

And speaking of dancing, he'd wanted to give her a big hug and a hot kiss after her Irish jig. Cute as hell. Sexy, too. Maybe someday....

Should he have mentioned Penelope? Maybe not, but when Fiona had wanted to change her elf name, he'd been hit with a wave of nostalgia. His kid sister had gone trick-or-treating as Galadriel several years in a row. She'd grown her blond hair to her waist so she'd look more like the elvish queen. He missed Penny. Time to make the phone call he owed her.

By the time he reached the tailgate, Fiona was already there, lowering it for him. He spotted the bag easily since it was right next to the empty space left by the Emerson delivery. This one was lighter than theirs since it only held three gifts and the plush moose.

Thank God Ben had the foresight to tuck a moose for each kid in the bags so they had something to hold onto while they waited for the big day. Some older kids might think they were too mature for a stuffed moose. But when they weren't used to getting anything, that little moose would likely be a big hit.

"Georgie Warner," Fiona prompted him. "His mother is—"

"Mrs. Warner?" He closed the tailgate and hoisted the bag over his shoulder.

"Correct." She laughed. "But it might not always be the case."

"Just let me know. Ben thinks it sounds better if Santa addresses the adults by their last name. But he's on a first-name basis with the kids."

"Makes sense." She smiled. "Ready, Santa?"

"Ready, Galadriel." Such a sunny, relaxed smile. He'd seen it a few times during the party after the auction and again when he'd driven her home that night. Not so much during their awkward date.

Mrs. Warner had brought Georgie out on the front porch. She looked young, maybe because her brown parka was way too big and her dark hair was pulled up in a high ponytail.

Georgie wore a Western-styled Santa suit complete with cowboy boots and a kid-sized Stetson. She bounced him up and down in her arms and sang to him as Leo and Fiona approached. It wasn't working. The dark-haired little boy regarded them with suspicion.

In response, Leo toned down his jolly greeting and paused at the foot of the porch steps. "Merry Christmas, Georgie and Mrs. Warner. I brought my favorite elf from the North Pole, Galadriel."

"Thank you so much for coming. See, Georgie? It's Santa and his elf. I'll bet she helps make the toys!"

"Yep, I do, and guess what's in the sack, Georgie? Toys for *you*."

He buried his face against his mother's neck. He knocked the hat askew, but the string under his chin kept it on his head.

"He's been so excited about having Santa visit," his mom said. "I guess the reality is a little overwhelming."

"We don't have to push it," Leo said. "We can just leave the gifts with you."

"Let's give him a little more time."

Time was in short supply, but that wasn't this young woman's fault. "Sure thing."

"I'm so grateful for the generosity of the community. I was laid off this summer and haven't found anything else that pays enough to afford a sitter. I love having more time with Georgie, but my savings won't last at this rate."

"That's gotta be tough." He lowered the bag to the porch steps. "Galadriel, if you'll unpack the bag, I'll stay right where I am so I don't startle Georgie."

"Got it, Santa."

"What kind of work do you do, Mrs. Warner?"

"I'm a receptionist, but I'd consider most anything that would cover my expenses."

"If I hear of an opening, I'll let you know." He already had some ideas. Henri might have even more.

"Thanks so much." She tilted her head toward a worn wicker chair on the porch. "I cleaned that chair before you came."

"Then Galadriel can put them on the chair, if you'd rather." He glanced at Fiona and she gave a quick nod.

"That's fine, but I was so hoping I could get a picture of Georgie sitting on your lap. A friend gave me this suit when her son outgrew it. Georgie will be too big for it next year, so if you'd sit there, maybe we can make it work."

"Yes, ma'am. It's worth a try." Treating the little kid like a skittish horse, he avoided looking at him as he climbed the steps. "Galadriel, would you please get out the little surprise we have for Georgie?"

"You bet, Santa."

"Did you hear that, Georgie?" Mrs. Warner jiggled him some more. "Santa brought you a *surprise.*"

Georgie ignored his mother and twisted in her arms to keep track of scary Santa. Leo sat in the wicker chair and gave the little boy a quick glance. The kid hid his face again.

Fiona climbed the steps, the moose in hand, her expression doubtful. Crossing to the chair, she gave him the moose with a look that clearly said *good luck.* Then she positioned herself by his side, her arm across the back of the chair.

"Oh, that's even better." Mrs. Warner came toward him holding Georgie. She'd managed to get his hat on straight but he'd started to squirm and whimper. "Santa and his favorite elf. Georgie, want to sit with Santa so momma can take your picture?"

The little boy struggled harder and shook his head.

Leo held up the moose. "This is for you, Georgie. It's Merlin the Moose. He wants to be your friend."

Georgie stopped struggling and turned to stare at the moose. Making a soft cooing sound, he reached out a chubby hand.

"He wants it," his mother said. "I'll give him to you and you can give him the moose."

"Yes, ma'am." It should have worked. He took the child into his arms, settled him on his lap and gave him the moose. Georgie's mother pulled her phone from her pocket.

But once Georgie had the moose, he began to kick to get free.

"Easy sport." Clark held him tighter, not wanting him to fall. The little boy tried to stand up and kicked harder. His pointed leather boots landed a punishing blow in a very sensitive spot. Leo gasped in pain.

"Up we go!" Fiona plucked Georgie neatly from his lap and held the wildly kicking kid in midair. "Mission accomplished, Mrs. Warner?"

"I got it! Great picture! Want to see it?"

"I'd love to," Fiona said, "but Georgie wants you, Mrs. Warner."

"Right. I'll take him, now." She shoved her phone in her pocket and grabbed him from Fiona. "Settle down, son. That's a good boy."

Fiona turned to face the wicker chair. "You okay, there, Santa?" She positioned herself so he had some privacy to catch his breath. "Just got an urgent message from Mrs. Claus." She held up her phone.

"Thanks." He sucked in air and pushed himself to his feet. "I'll... respond...in a sec. The presents..."

"Are stacked on the porch. I'll grab the bag."

He nodded and made his way toward the steps. "Merry Christmas to you, Mrs. Warner." He winced as he started down them. "And little Georgie."

"A Merry Christmas to you, Santa! I'll include this picture with the others when I send them to Ben on Christmas morning. You'll love it. It's a keeper."

"I'm sure." He walked to the truck with as much dignity as he could muster.

"Want me to drive?" Fiona murmured.

"I'll manage."

"Go on around the truck. I'll get myself in."

"Thanks." He made his way to the driver's side, pulled himself into the seat and settled down with a groan. "That kid has a kick like a mule."

"I'm so sorry. I—"

"You saved the day." He closed the door, buckled up, and started the engine. "If you hadn't picked him up, he would've scored again." He pulled away from the house. "Next?"

"Are you ready?"

"Hey, the show must go on, and the pain's letting up."

"Then continue down this road and take a left at the next four-way. Continue on for about three miles, take another left, and it's the first dirt road on the left."

"You're a lifesaver, Fi."

"I'm glad I'm here. Nobody should try to do this alone. It's a two-person—hey, Clark, I think we have snowflakes hitting the windshield."

"I thought I might be seeing spots in front of my eyes from the Georgie attack."

"Nope, it's snow, magical snow. Did you do that?"

"No, ma'am." He shifted in his seat. "Not much Christmas magic going on over here."

"Are you sure you don't want me to drive?"

"I'm sure. Can't have Santa chauffeured by an elf while he relaxes like some fat cat."

"Well, you are fat."

"I'm not fat. I'm fluffy."

"What's your padding made of?"

"Synthetic filling. You put it on like a vest with the opening in the back and tie it around the neck. Instant chubby."

"Sounds efficient. Are your glasses for seeing or for show?"

"Part of Ben's costume. He liked the look of the wire-rimmed specs, but the glass is clear. After the Georgie experience, I'm tempted to take 'em off. The next kid might try to punch me in the face."

"Let's hope not." She grinned. "Betcha didn't know this job requires a goalie mask and a cup."

He laughed. "I did not."

She turned to him. "Since you're recovered and we have a way to go, I'm calling in my raincheck from our earlier conversation. You said your parents wanted you to be famous. What for?"

He hesitated. Probably should reveal that sometime. "Acting. I was something of a child star. Did some teen movies, too. Hated it. Took me a while to realize I had a choice in the matter. I left when I turned eighteen."

"That doesn't sound like fun."

"Believe me, it wasn't."

"Were the teen movies comedies?"

"That's how they were billed. I didn't find them funny."

"I wonder if I saw one of them."

"Why do you say that?"

"Your laugh is so familiar. I've heard it before and I can't figure out where since I don't know anybody in town named Clark. Is that your real name?"

"Yep, sure is." He might need to quit laughing. Wasn't easy when he was with her. She tickled his funny bone.

Was he nervous about how she'd react when he told her who he was? Hell, yes. But they weren't there yet, and he had questions. "What were you supposed to be a professor of?"

"I toyed with the idea of becoming an Egyptologist."

"Yeah?

"I was fascinated by the pyramids."

"Were they built by aliens?"

"I so wanted to believe that when I was a kid, but I don't, anymore. The fact that convinced me was learning how they moved the stone."

"I've always wondered." He was loving this discussion. Sure would be fun to have talks like this cuddled by a fire. Talking and kissing.

"Turns out if you dampen sand, you reduce the friction and you can pull a loaded sledge way faster and easier than across dry sand. They've found evidence that's exactly what they did."

"Makes sense."

"Don't get me wrong. It's an amazing feat of architecture. But that's one key to the puzzle. They're finding new ones all the time."

"So why didn't you go into it?"

"Papyrus."

"The first paper?"

"Ah, but it's not! Then I found out the Chinese had paper way sooner. They even had— get this—toilet paper!"

"Well, shut my mouth." *And then kiss me.*

"Surprised the heck out of me, too. Anyway, I got hooked on the history of paper and then studied the environmental impact of it. I've always loved anything involving paper—books, stationery, journals. Selling recycled products so we can have the joy of it without wrecking the environment makes me happy."

"So the Chinese were the first. Who came next?" He already knew the answer. She'd told him during the drive home after the bachelor auction. That was when he'd vowed to get to know her better.

She launched into her favorite topic and he smiled. This was the Fiona he'd been looking for.

6

Fiona had gradually pieced together Clark's unfortunate past. Manipulated as a kid, Clark had rebelled the minute he'd come of age. Sounded like he might be estranged from his parents. She couldn't tell what the deal was with his sister Penelope, although he'd spoken of her with great affection.

He'd had it way rougher than she had. Her parents were disappointed but not controlling. Clark's story of being an instrument of his parents' ego could have made some men bitter, yet Clark had retained an innate kindness she admired.

And bonus, he could laugh about being kicked in the balls. He'd also liked her factoid about the pyramids and had asked good questions when she'd rattled on about paper.

Eventually she ran out of gas on that subject and switched topics. "What did Georgie's mother mean about sending pictures to Ben?"

"Since he doesn't get to see the kids open stuff, the parents send him pictures from Christmas morning."

"Oh, you know what? Beth said something about those pictures. I just forgot. That'll be fun to see. Except for the one of Georgie on your lap."

"Maybe she took it the second before he nailed me."

"She must have. She seemed oblivious to what he'd done. By the way, are you going to try and find her a job?"

"I'll see what I can do. I have some contacts."

"I wish I knew of something. I don't need anyone and neither does Beth. I wonder if she has any food service experience? There's Cup of Cheer, Gertie's and the Moose."

"I thought of those, too. I need to talk with her again. This wasn't the time to get into details."

"Especially after—"

"Yes, ma'am." He turned down a dirt road. At the end of it, light glowed through the bare branches of trees. "What's the intel on this one?"

She consulted the list. "Two boys, eight and six, Jay and Davey Hillman. Parents are Mr. and Mrs. Hillman. The dog's name is Scooby. He's friendly."

"I've met Scooby in town. Awesome dog." As he pulled the truck in front of a house with lights shining from every window, a gigantic German shepherd leaped from the porch, barking on the way around to the driver's side.

She sucked in a breath. "That's a friendly dog?"

"Oh, yeah, he's fine." Clark opened the door. "Hey, Scooby! How're you doing, boy?"

The dog woofed and wagged his tail as Clark stepped down and rubbed his head and behind his ears. "Who's a good dog? Who's the best dog ever? You are!" He scrubbed his gloved hands down Scooby's neck and along his spine, digging his fingers into the thick coat as the pooch wriggled in delight.

The lovefest going on between dog and man brought Clark into sharper, sexier focus. Did he have good pecs and a six-pack under that loose material and the Santa belly? Possible. Whenever he braked the truck, his thigh had tightened enough to glimpse muscle definition. Not that she'd been looking.

Yeah, right. She'd been paying more attention than she wanted to admit. Those broad shoulders filled out the Santa jacket nicely. The costume couldn't completely disguise his narrow hips and what was likely a firm backside. He might very well have a great body to go with his manly chin.

"We'll meet you by the tailgate," Clark called over his shoulder.

"Be right there!" Sitting in the cab musing about what was under Clark's Santa suit wasn't in her job description, now was it? Opening the door, she jumped out, phone in hand, and hurried to the back of the truck.

He'd already pulled down the tailgate and located the bag.

Scooby bounded toward her, clearly ready for her to continue what Clark had started. She put a tentative hand on his head.

"He's very gentle." Clark swung the bag over his shoulder.

"I'm not afraid. I just don't know much about dogs."

"He can tell. That's why he's standing there quietly. Very intelligent animal. Well-trained."

She stroked the dog's massive head as he gave her a solemn, brown-eyed stare. "Hey, Scooby. You're a very sweet dog."

"He'd let you do that all night."

Would you? She glanced up and caught him smiling at her. Whoa. If he'd deployed that sexy smile onscreen, no wonder his parents had seen dollar signs.

He cleared his throat. "We'd better get moving."

"Lead the way." Her stomach continued to flutter as she walked with him toward the house. Scooby switched his allegiance to Clark, trotting along right by his knee.

The boys came out wearing denim jackets, jeans tucked into cowboy boots and stocking caps pulled over their ears. Their parents, wearing similar outfits, followed their sons and stationed themselves behind the boys at the edge of the porch. Tall family. The kids looked a couple of years older than their ages on the list.

"Ho, ho, ho, Merry Christmas!" Clark called out.

The father pulled a harmonica out of his breast pocket and began to play as the mother and two boys sang *We Wish You a Merry Christmas.*

Clark paused, so she did, too. Scooby sat, ears pricked forward.

The little family poured so much enthusiasm into their song that Fiona's throat tightened. They might need some help from Santa this Christmas, but they'd give back as best they could.

When they finished, she clapped enthusiastically along with Clark. The kids executed bows and the proud parents grinned. Greeting the boys by name, Clark introduced her before they launched into distributing the gifts.

Jay, the oldest, whooped as he held up what was clearly a wrapped football. "I know what *this* is." Excitement rang in his voice.

"But you can't open it until Christmas," Clark said.

"I know. Mom and Dad told me that, too, but with this wrap job, it's obvious."

His little brother gave him a challenging glance. "But you don't know what *color* it is."

Jay laughed. "It's brown. They're always brown."

"Maybe not." Davey stuck to his guns. "You never know. You could be *so* surprised when it turns out to be yellow."

"Yeah, squirt." Jay gave him a tolerant smile. "A yellow football would be a surprise, all right."

Clark gave each of the boys their stuffed moose and the two immediately started butting the two plush animals' heads together in a mock battle.

Their father laughed. "Like I didn't see that coming. Hey, Santa, Scooby sure did take a shine to you."

Fiona checked on Scooby's whereabouts and he was sitting right beside Clark, gazing up at him with adoration.

Clark reached down to scratch behind the dog's ears. "I've taken a shine to him, too. You have a great dog."

"He's amazing, and he likes people, but I've only seen him act this devoted toward one other person besides us, a guy we meet sometimes in town. Scooby bonded with him right away. He's a wrangler who—"

"Yeah, I've seen that guy with your dog. Thought it was great. I'm honored that Scooby's giving me the same treatment. By the way, I sure appreciated the musical greeting. You're talented with that harmonica."

"Thanks. I'm teaching the boys. Jay's not too keen on it, but Davey's picking it up. It's handy to have a musical instrument you can stick in your pocket."

The discussion about harmonicas had the potential to go on indefinitely. Fiona glanced at her phone. Time to call this one. "Just got a text from Mrs. Claus, Santa."

"Let me guess," the dad said. "She wants you to pick up a loaf of bread on your way home."

Clark grinned. "Exactly. Ready to go, Galadriel?"

"Ready." Picking up the empty bag, she called out a quick *Merry Christmas* and hurried over to him. She kept her voice down as she walked back to the truck with him. "I didn't start timing this visit until after the song, but—"

"That's fine. But we need to keep the timing thing going or we'll never make it."

"I know. It's just that each stop is special in its own way."

"I agree. Leaving is the hardest part." He opened the door for her.

Climbing in, she tossed the bag in the back seat with the others. The names on the list stretched out, taunting her. They had to get faster at this. She checked the location on the next few stops.

Clark did his running board shout of *Merry Christmas to all and to all a good night* before sliding behind the wheel and closing the door. "What next?"

"Good news. These first three are on the outskirts of town and spaced far apart. Now we'll hit clusters of stops where we only need to go a block or two between each one. That should speed things up."

"Great." He buckled his seatbelt and started the truck. All business, now, he turned the truck around and started back to the main road.

She reeled off the details of the next location and the kids he could expect there.

"Got it."

She could fall in with his get-'er-done mentality, but the last stop had left her with questions. She wanted answers. "Clark..."

"What?"

"Something's not adding up. You weren't meeting Scooby for the first time. You told me when you opened the door that you'd met him in town. I think you're the wrangler Mr. Hillman was talking about."

"I am, but on this trip, I'm supposed to be Ben."

"For the kids, yes. For the adults, it's not such a big deal. Why didn't you say you were that person?"

"For the kids' sake."

"They weren't paying attention. They were involved in a moose battle."

He hesitated.

"Look, you said your name is actually Clark, and I believe you, but I'm starting to question the Smith part of it."

"Fiona, I—"

"You probably are Clark, and it could be like Marilyn's birth name was Norma Jean."

"It's not the same—"

"What I'm trying to say is this. If you're a bigger star than you want me to know, if you're hiding out in Apple Grove to get away from the paparazzi as well as your parents, that's fine. If you've chucked fame and fortune to be a wrangler on a ranch here, I get it."

"You're partly right."

"I thought so."

"But there's more to it than that."

"You don't have to tell me. We can just enjoy this one magical night with the snow falling and the carols playing on your phone and the kids eagerly waiting for us to bring them toys."

"You paint a lovely picture."

"Thank you."

"But I don't believe for one second that you'll rest until you solve the mystery. Galadriel wouldn't let it go and neither will you."

"Normally you would be right, but in your case—"

"Besides, I never intended this to be an unsolved mystery."

"Oh?" She twisted in her seat to stare at him. "You had intentions about tonight?"

"Yes, ma'am."

Her brain stalled. "What were they?"

"To reveal who I am over pie and hot cider."

"Wow, that's dramatic." And unsettling.

"Believe me, it isn't the route I would have chosen. But desperate times call for desperate measures."

"Desperate?" Her uneasiness grew.

"That may be a slight exaggeration."

"I should hope so. In any case, we do need to step up the program with these deliveries. We can't let ourselves be slowed down so much by cute kids, lovable dogs and harmonica-playing dads."

"Right."

"I won't distract you with pyramids and the evolution of paper, either."

"We had travel time to fill. That wasn't—"

"Maybe you drove slower."

"I might've. Talking to you is fun."

The compliment put her on alert. Had he asked for this job before or after Ben had chosen her to be the elf? Was this a setup? The blind date to end all blind dates?

Now that he'd admitted a plan to reveal his identity at the Choosy Moose, she questioned his motives for taking the job, although he clearly loved doing it. She might be icing on the cake.

This wasn't the time to sort it out, though. They had presents to deliver. But when that was done, she wanted answers. And not necessarily in a public setting.

7

Showtime. Leo focused all his energy on emptying the truck bed before nine. The proximity of the houses scheduled for a delivery helped enormously. Discussions with Fiona were short and to the point.

She was too smart to waste her breath on questions that would be answered once they were face-to-face at the Choosy Moose. By some miracle he'd made it through three toy deliveries before she'd questioned him about his identity.

Evidently she'd accepted that a reveal in the middle of spreading Christmas cheer could louse up the schedule. The tension of keeping this secret from her was getting to him, though.

After the last bag was delivered, he texted Ben to let him know they'd finished on time. Then he drove toward the town square and the Choosy Moose, relieved that he'd finally be able to come clean.

The place was jumping and parking along the Moose side of the square was out of the question. He glanced at Fiona. "Mind if I leave Ben's truck in front of your shop and we walk over?"

"I was going to suggest that. It's a madhouse. We'll be lucky to get a table. But I'm okay with sitting at the bar."

"Oh, we'll get a table. Ben reserved a two-top by the dance floor for nine-fifteen. It'll be available or heads will roll."

"By the dance floor?" She didn't sound thrilled with the news.

Ben had suggested it, hoping that after the first shock, Fiona would agree to dance with him. In Ben's mind, a few dances and maybe a few drinks would get them past the awkward stage. "We can ask for different seating when we get there."

"How about just telling me now? I'm not good with being surprised when I'm in the spotlight."

"I guess I could tell you before we go in." He should have nixed Ben's idea. Ben was a showman who believed in the grand gesture. His reasoning had made sense for someone like Henri, but not for Fiona. He pulled into a diagonal parking space in front of her shop. "Would you rather skip going to the Moose?"

"I'd like to go. It's a nice way to finish off the evening. But—"

"Then let's have our conversation here." Anxiety churned in his gut. He'd counted on being able to see her face and judge her reaction. The Moose was a happy place full of light, laughter and maybe forgiveness.

Sitting in the cab of Ben's truck had none of that. Maybe he could engineer a compromise. "On second thought, let's take a walk, head over to the gazebo."

"It's snowing."

"I know." He glanced at her. "What's a little magical snow between friends?"

She met his gaze in the dim light. "I'm game."

"Then let's do it. Listen, if you'll sit tight for a sec, I'd like to divest myself of the Santa belly before we head over there."

She gave him a smile. "Okay."

"I'll be around to get you in no time." Climbing out of the truck, he closed the door and moved to the cab's back door. Nobody was around to notice as he took off the Santa jacket. He draped it over the rim of the truck bed.

As he started to untie the Santa belly, the wind picked up and the snow fell harder and thicker, pelting his bare skin. He wrenched the door open, tossed the padded vest inside and slammed the door. Shaking snow off the jacket, he put it on, belted it and checked the pocket. The plush moose he planned to give her was still tucked inside.

His teeth chattered as he walked around to the passenger door. When he opened it, a gust of wind whirled snow into the cab. "I'm rethinking this plan."

"I figured." She grabbed her coat as he helped her down. "There's a thin line between magical snow and a blizzard. Let's go into the shop. You can tell me the big news there."

"All right." At least he wouldn't have the truck's console between them. He did his best to shield her from the icy blast as they hurried across the sidewalk to the shop's entrance.

She sucked in a breath. "I'm *freezing*." Twisting the key in the lock, she shoved open the door and scurried into the dim interior.

He followed, pushed the door closed and faced her, heart pounding. This was it. He'd lead with the plush moose.

"Better lock the deadbolt, Clark. When the wind's this strong, it'll blow the door open. I learned that the hard way. Lost some inventory."

Pivoting, he engaged the lock. Then he took a slow swallow as he turned back to her and reached in his pocket. "Fiona, I—"

"Do you want to come upstairs?"

He nearly choked. "Come upstairs?"

"Wait, wait. I didn't mean it like I think you just took it."

"I didn't—" He cleared his throat. "I didn't take it that way."

"The heck you didn't. I can't see your face very well in this light, especially when you're wearing those glasses, but I guarantee your eyes bugged out."

"I'll admit you startled me."

She took a breath. "Just for kicks, what if I *had* meant it that way?"

Dear God, how to answer? "I...um...well, I—"

"Never mind. That was unfair. I could be insulted either way."

"That was my thought." He exhaled. "And insulting you is the last thing I want to do."

"I only suggested it because standing in the dark while we have this discussion seems silly. I have a nice sitting area upstairs."

The longer he stood in the shadows, the more he liked unburdening his conscience here instead of under bright lights. She'd made the right call. "This won't take long. If we're still on good terms after I've had my say, we can just leave and head on over to the Moose."

"You think I might get upset?"

Way to go, dude. "Not necessarily. And I'd like to take you over to the Moose as planned. It's part of the experience."

Her gaze moved to the shop window where snow hit the glass like buckshot. "Mother Nature seems to have a different idea."

"It might let up."

"And what if we're not on good terms?"

"Let's think positive."

"But if we're at odds, the pie and cider plan doesn't sound very—"

"True. We can skip it. I'll drive Ben's truck to the parking area behind the bar, trade his vehicle for mine, and head home."

"Where is home?"

"You'll know that in a minute, but first I want you to have this." He held up the moose. "You get a Merlin, too."

"Aww!" She took it and held it against her cheek. "Have you been carrying Merlin around the whole time?"

"Had to. He's little and could get lost." At least that move had made him some points.

"Are you sure Merlin's a *he*? Just about every name these days can be either."

He smiled. "And checking underneath is no help. Gender neutral down there. Decision's up to you."

She gazed at him. "You're not using your Ben voice anymore."

"No, ma'am." His heart rate picked up. "Time to be me." After stuffing his gloves in his pocket, he put the glasses in there, too.

"I've heard that voice before."

"Yes, you have." He pulled off the stick-on eyebrows and took off the hat, which went in the other pocket. Last of all, he unhooked the beard from around his ears and crammed that in his pocket, too.

She stepped closer, peered up at him and gasped. "*Leo?*"

"Yes, ma'am."

She moved back so fast she bumped into a display table of boxed stationery. "You told me your name was Clark!"

"Because it is. My birth certificate says Clark Leopold Marston."

"There's no Smith in there, I'll bet."

"No, that was a cheat, but it seemed like a somewhat fair one. Nobody's named Smith."

"No, *everybody's* named Smith. That's why crooks use it for an alias. And sneaky cowboys."

Ouch. "Fiona, I was out of options. I just found out last night why you won't date me, so I asked Ben if—"

"You dreamed this up last *night*?

"Late last night, to be exact, after the Brotherhood wrapping party at the Moose. On the way home, I pleaded with Nick to tell me why you never—"

"He didn't tell you before? I thought for sure—"

"He didn't say anything because he figured there was nothing I could do about it. And there wasn't, except for this. It gave me one night to—"

"Does Ben know?" The pace of her breathing picked up.

"He does, but if you're upset, please don't blame him. I convinced him that he'd be doing us both a huge favor."

"Oh, did you, now?"

"Because I believe it. You've just spent more than three hours with me. Did you have fun?"

"Yes, but—"

"Are my looks really that big a deal?"

"You look like a movie star!"

"You knew that when you bid on me."

"Fair enough. I bid on you to challenge myself, take another step out of my comfort zone. Turns out it was a giant leap out of my comfort zone. You're so handsome I can't think straight. Literally."

"My looks are a curse, not a blessing. Early this year I gave up dating. Want to know why?"

"You were tired of women throwing themselves at you?"

"Yes, because I appeal to the ones who are fixated on appearance. I was afraid you'd be the same, but you weren't. Made me so happy. But now—"

"Attractive men, I'm fine with. I'm attractive, too. But when—"

"You're beautiful, Fi."

"Not like *you*. When I see that face, when I gaze into those blue eyes, I'm overwhelmed. I don't know what to say, what to do."

"You're holding your own right now."

"Because I can barely see you, especially now that I'm way over here. And you're wearing a baggy Santa suit."

"I could wear baggy clothes."

"You can't work in baggy clothes. They'd catch on things. You need those snug jeans and those sexy shirts that make your shoulders look a mile wide."

"I have a couple of ugly ones, a dirt tan and pea-green plaid and a barf brown and gray striped. They were on sale at Jeans Junction. They're hideous. If I—"

"Stop. You could wear the ugliest shirt sold in that store or in the entire *world* and you'd still turn my brain to mush. I don't like it when that happens. I don't like feeling like an idiot."

"But you're not an idiot. I was all set to talk about Pluto on our date and you cut yourself off."

"I was too distracted to discuss it intelligently. I would have started babbling nonsense."

"You didn't babble nonsense on the way home from Ed's party. We had a great discussion."

"About what? I was a little bit... toasted."

"Paper."

She groaned. "And I rambled on about it again tonight. You must think that's all I talk about. How embarrassing."

"Don't apologize. I enjoyed every minute."

"Sure you did."

"Damn it, I like that you're smart and you know stuff. Turns me on when you bring up subjects like how the Egyptians built the pyramids."

"Are you kidding?"

"No! That was the whole point of this, to prove that you could have fun with me, that we could enjoy interesting discussions. And unless I'm a bad judge of such things, we had chemistry tonight."

"I had chemistry with Clark Smith."

"Which is me."

"No, it's not. Clark Smith is jolly Saint Nick. You're Leo Marston, smokin' hot cowboy. Too hot to handle."

He sighed and ran his fingers through his hair. "So I take it we're not going over to the Moose for pie and cider?"

"Definitely not. The minute I see you in full light, I lose thirty IQ points. Maybe forty."

"And you still won't go out with me?"

"That's right."

Time for a Hail Mary pass. "Then this is it, the last time we'll spend time alone together?"

"Leo, I can't relax and be myself when I'm with you. I wish I could, but—"

"Will you let me kiss you goodbye?"

"What for?"

"To end the evening on a friendly note. We could shake hands, but considering you saved me from a little kid who was assaulting my manhood, I think we've moved past a stuffy handshake."

"I suppose."

"I've been thinking about kissing you ever since our date back in August, when it was clear you didn't want that. I've just spent the past three and a half hours thinking about it and hoping this time you would let me kiss you. Give a guy a break."

She hesitated. "I guess that's fair."

Not really. He had no intention of playing fair. Too much was at stake.

8

Fiona pressed her hips against the display table. Her legs shook and might not hold her up, so Leo would have to come to her. Besides, the shadows were deeper over here and the less she absorbed of his classic beauty, the better.

She'd spent the entire evening with Leo Marston. Hadn't had a clue. Sure, he was a professional actor, but she should have figured it out.

The California connection was an obvious tipoff. Ben had mentioned he worked with horses. Another big tell. His laugh had sounded familiar because he'd done a lot of it at Ed's party. She'd had an excess of champagne that night, but still.

He moved toward her, pausing before he was within kissing distance. She dragged in a nervous breath. Citrus. "You wore a different cologne tonight."

"Borrowed this from Garrett. Thought you might recognize my regular one."

"I would have. Yours reminds me of a rain-soaked forest."

"Did you like it?"

"Yes." Air was in shorter supply with every passing second. "I can't believe you went through all this for—"

"Because you don't know me very well."

"Clearly." He came closer. Her pulse skyrocketed.

"I was into you from the moment we met at the auction. I thought we had promise. I still do."

The space between his body and hers shrank again. She grasped at the shreds of sanity left to her. "Because you don't know me very well, either."

"But I wanted to. I thought we were off to a great start."

Only inches separated them. His breathing was as shaky as hers. Small consolation.

He gently removed her stocking cap and set it on the boxes of stationery stacked behind her. Taking her coat from her hand, he laid it on the table, too. His body brushed against hers.

She quivered in anticipation.

"We did have a nice time that night, Fi." His voice dipped to a seductive murmur. "A few laughs at the party, a little dancing, easy conversation on the drive home."

She gulped. "It was the champagne."

"Well, then, maybe—"

"Booze is the answer?"

"No, that's a bad idea."

"You think?"

"Tell you what." He slid his hand through her hair and cupped the back of her head as his voice roughened. "Let's stop thinking for a couple of minutes."

"Two minutes?" She panicked. "That's a long—"

"It'll go by fast." Tilting her head back, he leaned down and settled his mouth over hers.

Even though he'd taken his time leading up to it, she was woefully unprepared. She gasped at the velvet touch of his lips.

He lifted his head. "Easy. It's just a kiss."

And the Grand Canyon was just a ditch. The instant he'd made contact, she'd been jolted to her toes. Chemistry? How about nuclear fusion?

"Fiona? Are you—"

"Again." She grabbed his head in both hands and pulled him down. Maybe she'd been wrong. Maybe it wasn't so...oh, yes, it *was*.

With a groan, she wound her arms around his neck and abandoned herself to the fireworks. The velvet pressure of his lips against hers inspired her to shoot right past the getting-to-know-you phase and head straight for reckless abandon territory.

When he thrust his tongue into her mouth, she returned the favor. She might have whimpered. And plastered her body against the rock-hard body under the Santa suit.

That soft polyester hid nothing. This supposed goodbye kiss was all about hello. He had her trapped against the display table. Fine with her. One sweep of his arm would clear the merchandise and create a level surface.

Heat sluiced through her body and moisture gathered between her thighs. His kiss deepened and she wiggled closer, daring him to get rid of the boxes on the table so he could make use of the package firmly wedged between her thighs.

He lifted his mouth from hers. "This can't go anywhere."

"It's already gone around the moon and back."

His laughter was strained. "No kidding. Damn, Fi."

"Damn, Leo." She cleared the lust from her throat. "If this is a goodbye kiss, I'm Mickey Mouse."

"I want to take you upstairs. I can't. I don't have—"

"I should hope not." She sucked in air. "That would be creepy, Santa packing condoms."

"Creepy or not, I wish I had—"

"Kiss me again."

With a groan, he granted her request. In the process, he set every atom in her body ablaze. She took liberties, unbuttoning his jacket and slipping her hands inside to stroke his heaving chest. Sculpted, warm, heart thumping against her palm. Yum.

He cupped her backside, bringing her in even tighter. He had impressive equipment. But then he would. He was Leo Marston. And despite the voice of reason yelling at her that making love with him was a huge mistake, she was ready to risk it.

With a frustrated moan, he ended the kiss. "I can be back here in under an hour. If that's okay."

She gulped. "It's snowing hard. I don't want you going out in—"

His kiss cut her off and destroyed what was left of her brain power.

When he came up for air, she'd lost all modesty. "Stay here. There are other ways we can—"

"I want it all."

"The roads—"

"Aren't a problem." He kneaded her backside, arousing her, taking her beyond all resistance. He struggled to breathe. "I've been driving these roads for years."

"But—"

"I'm good at it."

"I'm sure you are." And she didn't mean driving in snow.

His answering chuckle was low and sexy. "Now you're talkin'. I'll be back before you know it."

"Okay. I'll give you my key. Just come upstairs. The bedroom's to the left. I'll be waiting."

"With the light on?"

Scary. Exciting, but still scary. "No lights, please."

"Fine with me. It can be black as pitch and I'll find you. I'd make love to you underwater if I had to."

"Underwater?"

"Yeah, wouldn't work, but I'd try to make it work. I want you so much I can't think straight."

"Me, either. One more kiss."

He captured her mouth, his heat calling to her, driving her insane. He kissed her until her breath came in ragged gasps.

He was in no better shape when he released her and backed away. "The sooner I leave, the sooner I'll be back."

"Right." She turned, grabbed the coat he'd laid behind her and fished the key out of the pocket. She held it out. "See you soon."

"Count on it." Pocketing the key, he buttoned his jacket, turned and strode out the door.

She sank against the table, quivering. If Leo made love the way he kissed, she was in for a night she'd never forget.

9

Leo accomplished the truck transfer in record time. Retrieving the Santa belly from the back, he took it with him. He'd have everything cleaned before returning it to Ben.

Ideally he would have folded all the gift bags. With a silent apology to Ben, he left them scattered all over the back seat. The evening hadn't turned out to be neat and tidy, with pie and cider followed by dancing to holiday tunes performed by an excellent country band.

He wasn't complaining.

For about two seconds he considered the condom dispenser in the men's bathroom at the Moose. But Santa slipping into the men's room to operate that dispenser was—to use Fiona's expression—creepy. And he'd rather trust the brand he had in the drawer under his bunk.

The wind howled around his truck as he climbed in the cold cab. He dug the Santa hat out of his pocket and put it on. Better than nothing. Leaving the parking lot, he headed out of town.

Fiona was right about the road. It was dicey and would get worse. How long did he dare stay with her? One hour? Two? Was she taking a shower while he made the round trip? Too bad he couldn't—

The wheel jerked as he hit a drift at the side of the road. He wrestled the truck back onto the pavement. Damn! *Focus, Marston.*

Jaw set, he forced himself to concentrate on the road ahead. One mile. Two miles. Three miles. *Just do it. Get there and back in one piece, okay?*

Four miles. Five miles. Not a soul was on the road in either direction. When had this stupid trip become so long? Had the swirling snow made him miss the turnoff?

Ah! There it was. He slowed the truck and swung wide to give him plenty of room. Now was not the time to slide right off the edge. Getting stuck would put a pitiful end to this amazing opportunity.

He didn't meet anybody on the ranch road, either. Buckskin folks stayed home on a night like this because they were blessed with common sense. The prospect of making love to Fiona had destroyed his.

After parking in front of the bunkhouse, he battled his way to the front door, wrested it open and quickly closed it once he was inside.

Garrett glanced up from a book he'd been reading while lounging next to the wood stove with a bottle of cider and a bowl of chips. "That Santa outfit isn't up to this weather."

"Luckily we got it done before the storm hit."

"That's good."

"I'm changing clothes and going back to town."

Garrett closed the book. "What?"

"Fiona invited me upstairs."

"Then why the hell did you drive back here?"

"Condoms."

"But the Moose has—"

"I decided against those. Go back to your book. I'll be gone in five." He walked to his bunk, took off the Santa hat and tossed it on the wool quilt he'd bought at a craft fair. He wasted no time getting out of the Santa suit.

Garrett left his seat by the wood stove and perched on the opposite bunk. "You know you could end up in a ditch and freeze to death."

"Totally worth it." He put on socks and pulled on a clean pair of jeans.

"That's only if it happens on the way home. If you die on the way—"

"I won't." He grabbed a shirt, the tan and pea-green one for good measure, and shoved his arms into the sleeves. "I'm focused."

Garrett sighed. "That's what they all say. Then the highway patrol finds the nose of your truck buried in a snowbank and your cold dead corpse huddled in the cab."

"Thanks for the vote of confidence." He buttoned the shirt and tucked it into his jeans. Under these circumstances, no need for a belt.

"Damn it, Leo, don't drive back there. If she said yes tonight, she'll say yes again tomorrow night and the roads will be plowed."

"It's a miracle she said yes tonight." He sat on the bunk and reached for his boots.

"You gotta tell me why she did. I don't expect to ever see you again."

"Oh, for God's sake. I'm not going to die." After tugging on the boots, he stood.

"Especially if you give up this radical idea and stay here."

"Can't do it. This window of opportunity could close at any minute." He grabbed his lined denim coat from a peg on the wall.

"How'd you open it?"

"Hail Mary pass. One of Charley's moves." Crouching, he opened the drawer under his bunk and took out a couple of condoms.

"That guy casts a huge shadow."

"Yep." Leo shoved the condoms in his pocket. "He told us whenever he got crossways with Henri, he'd abandon the argument and kiss her senseless."

"The Hail Mary pass?"

"Exactly." He crammed his work Stetson on his head. Fancy didn't cut it with this woman. "First time I ever tried it, but it works like a charm."

"Then you can try it again tomorrow night." Garrett left the bunk and blocked his path. "Don't do this, Leo. Since the Brotherhood isn't here, I have to be the one to convince you this is insane."

"Sure it is." He looked Garrett in the eye. "And that's what makes it fun. Stand aside."

Garrett held his gaze. "She must be something special."

"She is."

"Then good luck, buddy." Garrett squeezed his shoulder before moving to let him pass. "Got your phone?"

Leo held it up as he continued toward the door.

"Call me if you get in trouble. I'll be there."

Glancing over his shoulder, Leo gave him a smile. "Thanks, bro."

Garrett blinked. "But I'm not—"

"In my mind you are. We just need to make it official." Touching two fingers to the brim of his hat, he opened the door and walked into the teeth of the storm. Fiona was waiting.

* * *

The harrowing drive was taking more time than he'd estimated. With no one ahead of him, he couldn't follow taillights and tire tracks. He took it at a snail's pace so he wouldn't go off the road. He used the map function on his phone to gauge the distance.

What if Fiona was getting worried? Easing to a stop, he engaged the hand break and put on his blinkers in case anyone came up behind him.

Then he texted Fiona. *On my way. Slower than expected due to heavy snow.*

She replied immediately. *Where are you?*
Halfway.
Point of no return?

He smiled. *Passed that when I kissed you and you kissed me back.*

Take care of yourself.

I will. Setting the phone in the cup holder, he released the hand brake and started forward. Snowflakes created a starburst pattern against his windshield. The wipers scraped it off.

The sense of isolation in a snow-bedazzled world crept over him gradually. He didn't acknowledge the power of so much whiteness until he became disoriented, no longer convinced he was moving in the right direction despite the evidence on his phone.

Another text from Fiona. *Call me if you can.*

Stopping a second time, he put on the blinkers again and made the call. "What's up?"

"The storm's knocked out power to the entire square."

"Wow. Are you set with candles and a flashlight?"

"My flashlight's on my phone and the battery's getting low. I have two holiday pillar candles, but they're Christmas presents for Beth and Eva."

"Can you buy two more before Christmas?"

"I doubt it. I got them from a local lady at the Christmas craft fair."

"I have a flashlight in the truck and I'll charge my phone on the way in." He reached into the console and hooked up his phone to the truck's auxiliary outlet before turning off his blinkers and starting back down the road.

"Good thing one of us is prepared. The Moose must have a generator. Some light's coming from over there."

"They have one. Have to with all the perishables in the food locker."

"How long could the outage last?"

"Hard to say. Is this your first one since you moved here?"

"There was a storm-related one last winter, but it only affected my side of the square. I've never seen it all go dark."

"I'm sure they're working on it. I'll be there soon. How's the temperature in the apartment?"

"Dropping."

"Maybe we can do something about that."

_10_

Maybe we can do something about that.

Fiona had laughed at Leo's comment and thrown back a saucy _who needs central heat, right?_ Yeah, Fiona Hildebrand was exchanging sexy banter with Leo Marston, the hottest thing since sliced pizza.

She didn't trust herself to keep it up, so she used her phone's low battery as an excuse to end the call. "But contact me if you have any issues!" she added quickly.

"You'll be the first one I contact. I don't want you to worry."

"That's very sweet."

"Give me a chance and I'll show you how sweet I can be."

"Gonna give me a sugar high?" Hey, another flirty remark. They were way easier to deliver on the phone.

"A sugar high, a contact high, whatever you want, Fi. I'm there for you."

"Can't wait. Better disconnect before my phone goes belly-up." _And combusts._

"See you soon."

"I'll be here." She tapped the disconnect button and sagged against her couch cushions, her heart racing. Ready or not, she would soon be naked with Leo.

He was defying the elements so he could make love to her. Why was he so determined? Was it the novelty of being refused? He likely wasn't used to that.

She hadn't meant to present him with a challenge, but maybe she accidentally had. That could help explain his single-minded pursuit. But what level of sexual satisfaction would justify driving through a blizzard?

As the minutes ticked by, she paced the compact apartment, her furry slippers whispering against the wooden floor. At least she'd taken a shower before the hot water heater stopped working. She'd changed the sheets on her bed before the lights had gone out.

She had no sexy nightgowns, despite being close friends with Beth, who owned Racy Lace. She'd put on her red chenille robe, which was soft, warm and felt good against her skin.

Was there something else she should be doing in preparation for a man who represented her idea of male perfection? At least his chiseled features wouldn't be an issue in a blackout.

Without the mellowing effect of liquor, she was mesmerized by Leo fully dressed. Undressed? She envisioned a well-endowed version of Michelangelo's *David*. He wanted to be accepted as a normal, flesh-and-blood man. Could she do that?

A few minutes past midnight, a key turned in the lock downstairs. "Fi?"

She raced downstairs. "Oh, my God, you made it."

"I made it. I brought—"

She rushed into his arms, absorbing the cold from his jacket and tasting melted snow on his lips as he shoved back his hat and kissed her.

Something he was holding pressed against her back. He broke away. "Let me get rid of the flashlight." After setting it on the floor, he pulled her back into his arms with a groan.

Their kiss took a while. The more it heated up, the less she was inclined to move from this spot. His talented mouth and strong arms erased her anxiety and replaced it with eager anticipation. By the time he lifted his head, she'd softened like wax to a flame.

Breathing fast, he brushed his lips over hers. "Thought you were gonna wait in your bedroom."

"Not when you're driving through a blizzard. I—" The wind rattled the door. "Leo! The—"

He spun toward it, slammed his palm against the surface and twisted the deadbolt. "Damn." He turned back to her. "Forgot."

"So did I. Quick reflexes, there, mister."

"Thanks. Good thing we didn't go straight upstairs. You would have had a royal mess down here." Taking off his hat, he ran his fingers through his hair. "Once I start kissing you, I can't seem to stop. I just... forget everything else." He sounded bewildered by his lack of control.

"I'll take that as a compliment."

He was silhouetted against the faint glow coming from the Moose. "It's definitely a compliment." His tone softened. "Scares me some, too." A hint of vulnerability crept into his voice. "I've never..." Sighing, he shook his head. "I swear this isn't a line. The truth is, I've never felt like this."

"Maybe because I didn't call you back?" She said it gently but wanted to put it out there.

"That's not the reason."

"I doubt you're used to that reaction."

"I'm not, but—"

"I honestly didn't mean to present you with a challenge."

"I know you didn't. On the other hand, I've never worked so hard to..."

"Get a woman into bed?"

His shoulders hunched as if he'd winced. "I hope you don't think that's my only goal."

"Not your only one, but making love to me must be very important, or you wouldn't have driven through a blizzard to—"

"Point taken." He cleared his throat. "I'll admit I thought about it all the way here. I'm thinking about it now. I want you. I ache for you, Fi. But if I need to hold off to prove I care about more than sex... we can sit and talk, instead."

She blessed the shadows that hid her smile. "That wouldn't work for me."

He was silent for a moment. "Okay, if you want me to leave, I can probably make it over to Nick and Eva's place. They—"

"I don't want you to leave."

"You don't?"

"I want you to come upstairs and make love to me."

He exhaled. "Thank God." He started toward her and stopped. "I don't want to drip snow all over the place." Returning to the door, he leaned against it, took off his boots and left them on the doormat. Then he left his damp hat on top of his boots.

Finally he scooped up the flashlight. "Want this on?"

"Don't need it." She held out her hand. "I can make it upstairs blindfolded."

He laced his fingers through hers. "Then lead the way. But it'll be handy if we need it."

"I only have a queen. I think you'll be able to find me without a flashlight." She guided him to the back of the store.

He laughed. "Not crazy about the flashlight?"

"From what I could see, it's a big one."

"Yep. This baby can light up a room."

"But the universe has gifted us with a blackout. Don't you think that's interesting?"

"Sure, until I stub my toe."

"I'll make sure you don't."

"This thing has a dimmer switch. We could keep it turned down."

"But wouldn't you rather embrace the mystery of the darkness?" She started up the stairs.

"I'd rather embrace you without crashing into things."

"But then you're not really experiencing a blackout. Making love in total darkness." She couldn't wait.

"Never done that."

"Me, either, but I'm sure it's possible."

"How do you know?"

"Two blind people can make love."

"But they're used to the situation. Their other senses are more developed."

"This stairwell is very dark. You haven't stumbled once."

"I'm following your lead. And I can see a little bit in the light from the Moose. In your room I probably won't."

"You'll need to use your sense of touch, then, won't you?"

He sucked in a breath. "Okay. You have my attention."

"And taste." She shivered in anticipation.

"Mmm."

"And sound. Sound can tell you so much about... what's going on."

"I'm getting the idea." His grip tightened. "Do you have anything on under your bathrobe?"

"You'll find out, won't you?" She topped the stairs and started toward her bedroom.

"I hope you'll let me take it off."

"I will. But first I want to undress you."

"You do?"

"Well, duh."

"I should've known you'd have a plan."

"I've had time to think about this, too." Darkness enriched the sound of his voice, sending arrows of sensation pulsing through her. She led him into the bedroom and paused. "Where are the condoms?"

"What makes you so sure I have more than one?"

"If you drove through a blizzard and back for one condom, you're not the man I think you are."

"So I have more than one. Do you want to take charge of those?"

"It's logical. I know the room. I can put them in the bedside table drawer so we don't lose them."

"We're not losing them. I have a flashlight."

"We should put that somewhere safe, too. You'd better give it to me."

"Um, okay." He handed it to her with obvious reluctance. "Sure is dark. I can't see my hand in front of my face."

"Exciting, huh?"

"Yes, ma'am, in an unnerving sort of way."

"Stay right here while I tuck this away."

"Tuck it where, exactly?"

"Never mind."

"Is there a window in here?"

"I drew the curtains to keep in the heat." She opened the closet door and set the flashlight inside.

"You put it in a closet. Which is on my left. Must be a wall there."

"See? You're catching onto the tricks of operating in the dark. While I waited for you, I counted the number of steps between everything in this room."

"Which gives you home field advantage."

"I know."

His chuckle was low and sexy. "You're a fascinating puzzle, lady."

Heart pounding, she drew closer. "Do you like puzzles?"

"Always have." Reaching out, he gripped her arm and pulled her close. "Bring it on, Fi."

11

Love in the dark. Leo handed over the condoms and Fiona transferred them to the bedside table drawer, along with his phone. The rasp of the drawer came from the right and slightly in front of him. If he'd calculated correctly, she stood between him and the bed.

With all that pacing and planning she'd likely turned back the covers. His jeans pinched something fierce as she pushed his jacket from his shoulders and laid it... somewhere. Could be a chair or dresser to his left.

His hearing sharpened, focusing on the changes in her breathing and the brush of her fingers as she unbuttoned his cuffs. "I wore one of the ugly shirts."

"That's funny." Her voice had a smile in it.

"Yeah. Can't see it."

She took a shaky breath as she started down the row of buttons. "Thanks for the effort."

"Didn't figure..." He cleared the tension from his throat. "Didn't figure on a blackout."

"It's the thought that counts." She tugged the shirt from the waistband of his jeans and reached for the remaining buttons.

"Just pull it over my—"

"That's okay. I've got it." She finished with the buttons, slipped his shirt off and laid it wherever she'd put his jacket. "No T-shirt?"

"I run hot."

Her breath hitched. "Uh-huh."

He caught her hands and brought them to his lips. "I'm going crazy, Fi." He nibbled on the tips of her fingers. "Can you move a little faster?"

"I'll try. I'm... kind of shaky."

"Me, too." He placed her hands on the waistband of his jeans.

After unfastening the button, she worked the zipper down. He gritted his teeth as she edged past his aching cock. With no visuals to distract him, the needs of his package took center stage.

She paused. "Are you okay?"

"I will be. Keep going."

"Right." She pushed his jeans to his ankles and he stepped out of them. While she was down there, she pulled off his socks, too.

In the darkness that enveloped him, she was his touchstone. He was desperate to hold her. Grasping her by the shoulders, he drew her up. "I need to kiss you."

"I'm not fin—"

He captured her mouth, instinct guiding him when eyesight could not. The connection anchored him, filled him with energy and purpose. He'd never craved a kiss the way he craved Fiona's.

He pulled her close and the supple material of her robe caressed his bare chest. Sliding his hand to her waist, he loosened the sash. The robe parted. He pushed it off her shoulders and she let it fall.

Ah. Warm, silken skin. Plump breasts. Dizzy with anticipation, he cupped her breasts and squeezed gently. Her soft moan sent a signal straight to his privates. He lifted his mouth a fraction from hers. "Where's the bed?"

"Right behind me."

He guided her backward and she tumbled onto the mattress. He followed her down. Slowly massaging her breasts, he nuzzled the hollow of her throat. "Are we at the foot of it or the side?"

"The... side." Her breathing was even more ragged than his.

Good info. He'd reposition them in a minute. But first... cradling her warm breasts in his cupped hands, he trailed kisses from her throat to the taut nipple demanding his attention.

After a few swipes with his tongue, he began to suck. And Fiona came unglued, gripping his head and digging her fingertips into his scalp. The rich aroma of aroused woman encouraged him to slide a hand between her thighs.

She was drenched. Accepting the moist invitation, he pushed two fingers deep and began an intimate caress that soon had her writhing against the sheets.

He kissed his way back to her mouth. "Come for me, Fiona. Let go, pretty lady."

With a soft cry, she arched her back and abandoned herself to his touch. As her climax took hold in the velvet darkness, he longed for the light. Just enough to enjoy the rosy flush on her bare breasts, the pink on her cheeks, the glow of pleasure in her green eyes.

Panting, she sank back to the bed. "Wonderful." She gulped for air. "So good."

He feathered a kiss over her lips. "Only the beginning."

"Great... intro."

"Glad you liked it. Don't go away." Sliding off the bed, he stood and stripped off his briefs.

Sheets rustled. She was on the move. "I can get the—"

"Let me. I pinpointed the bedside table when you opened the drawer."

"Are you sure?"

"Yes." He took two steps to his right and banged his toe on something solid. "Found the table."

"Does it hurt?"

"The table's just fine."

"Your toe."

"Could've been worse." He explored the area directly in front of him and discovered a good-sized table lamp with a base of artfully positioned horseshoes. "Could've caught something important on your lamp."

"Yikes. I forgot about—"

"Dodged a bullet." He opened the drawer. "Glad I won't have to tell the doc I caught it on a horseshoe."

Muffled laughter was followed by a choked apology. "It's not funny."

"Sure it is." He tore open the condom and rolled it over his intact equipment. "Since it didn't happen."

"I was worried about your bare toes. I didn't think about your bare—"

"Which extends well beyond my toes."

"Clark Leopold Marston, are you bragging?"

"Just stating the facts." He turned toward the bed. "Where are you?"

"I'm here. Come find me."

He put his knee on the bed. "In the middle, or did you move all the way over? I don't want to accidentally—"

"Come find me." Her voice lowered to a soft purr. "Follow my voice. Come kiss me, Leo."

Climbing onto the bed and robbed of sight, he focused on her breathing. And her body heat. His skin prickled in awareness as he drew near. Her scent drove him wild. He adjusted his direction, leaned down and placed a kiss on her thigh.

"You missed."

"No, I didn't." Grasping her knee and coaxing it toward him, he kissed her again, this time on her inner thigh. "You didn't say where you wanted that kiss."

Her breath caught. "Guess not."

"Do you have a footboard?"

"No."

"Good." Moving between her thighs, he stretched out on his stomach, slid his hands under her firm tush and pulled her toward his waiting mouth. "I choose this spot." And he settled in.

Her quick gasp was soon followed by a soft cry of pleasure, then a deep throaty moan, the sound of a woman in a very happy place. In moments she was even happier. And calling out his name. He loved that part.

Her climax was a noisy affair with some salty language thrown in. Some laughter, too. He stayed where he was, savoring the taste of her until her breathing slowed and she stopped trembling.

"Hey." Her voice was soft and slightly hoarse. "Come here, you."

He trailed kisses up her body as he put himself in position for what his not-so-patient cock wanted. "What can I do for you, ma'am?"

She cupped his face in both hands and took a shaky breath. "I hesitate to say." She brushed her thumbs over his cheeks. "Your ideas are spectacular."

"Liked that, did you?"

"If you couldn't tell, you weren't paying attention."

"Oh, I was paying attention."

"I got a little... carried away."

"My favorite was when you started laughing."

"I couldn't help it! It felt so damn *good.* You know how when something is terrific and then it gets even better? And you just have to laugh because it's so amazing?"

"I'm not sure I do know."

"First time it's happened during sex."

"Oh?"

She chuckled. "You're smiling, aren't you?"

"Might be." Grinning like a fool was more like it. He'd given her a peak experience.

"I could hear it in your voice."

"Hm." Darkness. Who knew it could be so sexy?

She stroked his chest. "Your heart's beating fast."

"That's a fact."

"You said you wanted it all."

"So I did."

"I think it's time."

"Yes, ma'am." Dropping his hips, he probed once and pushed deep, sheathing himself in her warmth. He almost came. "Wow."

She swallowed. "That's... very nice."

"Understatement." He sucked in a breath and struggled for control. "I'll just... stay like this for a bit."

"Fine with me." She slid her hands down his back and cupped his ass. "Mm, *mighty* fine."

He choked on a laugh. "Thanks."

"Darkness rocks. I'm totally focused on you nestled inside me." Her core muscles tightened.

He gasped. "Fiona..."

"Let yourself come, Leo. Don't hold off like some macho guy. Enjoy yourself."

With a groan of surrender, he began to thrust. Cocooned with Fiona as the storm howled outside, welcomed by the moist tension of her warm sheath as he pushed deep again and again, he reveled in a world saturated with pleasure.

As the sensations intensified, she urged him on, rising to meet him, crying out for more. He plunged into her with abandon, letting the glorious friction stoke the fire until he couldn't hold back any longer.

Bellowing her name, he buried himself one last time and let go. Her climax milked his pulsing cock as he shuddered in the grasp of a spectacular release.

Reentry took a while. He gulped for air and trembled in the aftermath as the haze in his brain gradually cleared. "That was... incredible. Better than incredible."

"Sure was." She caressed his sweaty back with lazy movements of her hands. "I'm glad you didn't get tangled up with a horseshoe."

He laughed. "I've been waiting for that line."

"Really? How come?"

Leaning down, he gave her a soft kiss. "Just seems like a Fiona thing to say."

"Is that good or bad?"

"That's good. Very good."

12

"I'm in love with the dark." Fiona lay in a state of bliss, still snugly connected to Leo. "I've never felt this sexy in my life."

"And I love hearing that." He gave her another gentle kiss. "But now comes the unromantic part. I need to navigate a route to your bathroom to get rid of the condom."

"No worries. I'll take you."

"Sorry, not happening. There are some things—"

"We'll be in the dark. Trust me, it'll work out fine."

"That flashlight in the closet would work out fine, too. I'll dim it down and turn it off the minute I finish with this chore."

"You'll break the spell."

"Walking me to the bathroom will be a major spell breaker."

"No, it won't. When we get in there, I'll hand you my little wastebasket. Easy peasy."

"I like to wash up after—"

"I'll do it for you."

"I'd rather handle that myself."

"Why not let me handle it? A little warm water, a soft washcloth. Could be nice."

"Oh."

She smiled as their connection down below tightened a fraction. "Want to consider my plan?"

"Guess so."

"Then wait by the bed and I'll be your guide."

He eased away from her and the mattress shifted as he got up. "Do you want your robe? It's right here by my feet."

"No, thanks. Just nudge it aside." Rolling to the edge, she used his breathing to gauge where he was standing. She climbed out. "I'm on your left."

"I know. You're giving off lots of heat." He reached for her hand and wove his fingers through hers.

"You're not exactly cool, yourself, cowboy."

"Not surprising. I was recently plugged into an excellent heat source."

"And will be again." She squeezed his hand. "I'll head out the door first. Then we'll turn left. I'll take it slow."

"I assume you've counted the steps to your bathroom."

"You assume correctly." She started toward the door.

He followed behind her. "How big is the bathroom?"

"Small. Sink and toilet on the left as you come through, shower on the right."

"Ever done a trust walk, where you're blindfolded and someone leads you around?"

"When I was a kid."

"This reminds me of that. Although I wasn't naked."

"I won't let anything happen to you."

"And here I was hoping something *would*."

She laughed. "I meant nothing bad will happen to you. I'm stepping into the bathroom now. As you follow me, the tile will be cool on your feet."

"First cool thing since I walked into this apartment."

"Complaining?"

"No, ma'am."

"Stay there." She moved all the way to the back wall, picked up the small wastebasket and brought it to him, nudging his arm with the edge. "Here you go."

"Thanks."

"I'll scoot around you so I can get to the sink." She hugged the glass door of the shower stall so she wouldn't interfere with his task.

"Smells like peppermint in here."

"I have peppermint soap."

"For Christmas?"

"Yes. Beth gave it to me."

"You took a shower before I arrived, didn't you?"

"Uh-huh." She plucked a washcloth from the towel rack.

"Too bad I didn't have time to do the same."

"No worries. Got you covered." She closed the drain and turned on the left tap. "Oh, good. It's still hot."

"So am I." His arm came around her waist. "I heard something about warm water and a soft washcloth." He drew her hair back and nuzzled the curve of her neck.

The velvet brush of his mouth against her skin carried memories that made her quiver. "And that interests you?" She wrung some of the water out of the terry cloth.

"Very much." He nipped her shoulder.

"Step back a little. I need room to work."

He moved away and bumped against the glass door. "Found the shower."

"Come one step toward me."

His breath quickened as he moved closer. "Never thought I'd be so excited by a woman with a washcloth in her hand."

"No one's ever given you a sponge bath?"

"No one ever offered."

"Then let me be the first. I'll start with your chest."

"My chest? I thought you were planning to wash my—"

"Oh, I am. But I'll work up to it. Or rather, down to it. Hold still." She started with his pecs, slowly massaging the warm, damp cloth over his lightly furred chest.

He gave a low hum of pleasure.

"I thought you'd like this."

"Why?"

"Your choice when you climbed into bed. A man who decides to please a woman that way... it's a very sensual impulse." She put down the washcloth and pulled a hand towel off the rack, paying loving attention to his damp skin before dipping the cloth in the water again and wringing it out. "It indicates a very sensual nature."

"Says who?"

"All the authorities on sexual response."

"Name one."

"Too many to count." She began sponging off his taut abs.

He sucked in a breath. "You're making this up."

"Am I?" She put down the washcloth and picked up the hand towel.

"Yeah, and I don't care. That towel is soft, too."

"Organic cotton. Like it?"

He exhaled. "I do. Pretty soon you'll find out how much."

"The sponge bath is turning you on?"

"You knew it would."

"Maybe." The dark freed her to be more seductive than she'd ever dared. After dunking the washcloth in the water once more, she wrung it out and dropped to her knees.

His breathing rasped in the small space. When she made contact, he gasped.

"Too warm?"

His soft chuckle had a breathless quality. "Too good. Take it easy, please."

"I'll be gentle." He was fully erect, magnificent in his arousal. She wrapped the warm cloth around his considerable girth.

"And quick?"

"Maybe not *so* quick. I want you to enjoy the experience." She tenderly stroked the washcloth up, over and around his package.

"I'm enjoying." His voice was tight. "I just don't want to—" He gasped again as she paid special attention to more sensitive areas. "I should have brought the other condom. I want—"

"That's for later." She tossed the terry cloth on the counter, wrapped both hands around all that bounty, and licked moisture from the tip.

"Fi." His voice was hoarse. "I just wanted to... fool around. I didn't mean for you to...."

"But I did." She gripped him more firmly. "I intended to clean you up and have my way with you."

He gulped. "I should... stop you."

"Should I stop?"

"No." He shuddered. "God help me, I want you to."

"And I will." By a twist of Fate, she was grasping one of the most sought-after, free-range cocks in the county, probably in the state. She intended to give Leo the time of his life.

13

The moment Fiona took charge was a defining moment in Leo's life. Oral sex would never be the same. His attempt to keep his cool was a losing battle, mostly because of her unpredictable approach. If she had a playbook, it wasn't obvious. Her devotion to the task quickly robbed him of control and he came in an embarrassingly short time.

Her soft swallow humbled him. Drawing her to her feet, he kissed her slowly and thoroughly, letting her know without words that he'd loved every second. She'd raised the bar to impossible heights.

Then he took her hand. "Follow me. I'm taking you back to bed."

She resisted. "Don't you think I should lead us—"

"You're not the only one who can count steps." He tugged on her hand. "My turn to do the trust walk."

"I just don't want you to hurt yourself." She sounded doubtful.

"Trust me."

"Okay."

He managed the journey back to her bedroom without incident. Another night in this apartment and he'd have it down. But they hadn't talked about another night, had they?

He didn't want to talk about it now, either. Caressing, kissing, snuggling—that's all he cared to do for the time being. Rolling around with her on the rumpled sheets, he concentrated on the silken expanse of her skin under his fingertips, the heady aroma of desire, the husky tone of her voice, the taste of salt on her skin.

The chance to explore her eager body was a gift, one he'd nearly lost. He drew out the fooling around part because it was a fascinating adventure. Besides, he only had one condom left.

As a bonus to the make-out session, he discovered the spots where she was ticklish and the places where a light touch nearly brought her to orgasm. She wasn't shy about giving directions, either.

When he couldn't stand waiting another second, he made love to her again, savoring the increased richness as he deployed everything he'd learned so far... until his brain stopped working. With a groan of surrender, he submerged himself in the ecstasy that flowed between them in those final moments before they both let go.

Afterward, she lay with her head pillowed on his outstretched arm, her hand resting on his sweaty chest. "In case I didn't say it enough when I was coming, you're amazing."

"In case I didn't say it enough when I was coming, so are you."

"No more condoms, huh?"

"Sorry. I miscalculated."

"Maybe we should get some sleep so we won't be zombies in the morning."

"Probably should. Wind's letting up."

"Is it?" She lifted her head and listened. "You're right, although I can still hear the snow hitting the window." She nestled into the crook of his arm again. "What if you can't get back to the ranch to do... whatever you do there?" A touch of worry colored her words.

"I'll leave before it gets light, if that's what you're asking."

"I'm not. Well, not exactly. But if your truck's buried in—"

"I'm pretty good with a shovel."

"I'm sure you are, but I doubt you can shovel your way back to the ranch."

He laughed. "Not in time to do chores, anyway. But Apple Grove has the best road crew in the county. They're probably out there right now. I'll text Nick before I leave, see if he wants to drive tandem back to the ranch. We'll get there."

"Okay." She sounded relieved. "Thank you for going along with the blackout."

Clearly it wasn't a random comment. Was she wondering what came next? If so, he'd help her out. "Whatever works, Fi. If that means we meet in your darkened apartment at night, then I'm fine with it. Just so I get to keep making love to you."

Her breath caught.

Uh-oh. Maybe she didn't want that. He rolled to his side to face her, even though he couldn't see her face. "Fi?"

"You're... um, willing to keep doing this?"

"Willing and eager."

"Oh."

"That surprises you?"

"In a way. I didn't get my expectations up. You agreed to go along with the darkness routine tonight, but then I thought you'd want to move the action into the light."

Which he'd love, but clearly she wouldn't. He had a split second to choose his path. "But you're more relaxed in the dark."

"It's sort of unusual, though."

"No more unusual than a guy putting on a Santa suit so he could get to know you."

"Yeah, can't say I've ever heard of that before."

"I want to keep seeing you. Well, or not seeing you. I want to keep kissing you, touching you, making love with you. And I'd rather do it in a darkened room than wear an itchy beard and a Santa hat while we're getting it on."

She gave a little snort of laughter. "Now there's a picture." She took a breath. "What... what do you have in mind?"

"Sharing your bed as often as you'll have me. Under whatever conditions you set."

The seconds ticked by as he waited, nerves on edge.

At last she spoke. "Can we take it one day at a time?"

He exhaled. "Absolutely."

"Or rather, one night at a time."

"Right."

"Are you free tomorrow night?"

"Hell, yes."

She responded with a soft, sexy laugh. "Around eight?"

"I'll be here."

"You shouldn't have to battle a blizzard this time."

"No, ma'am." And he'd bring more condoms. "By the way, Garrett knows I drove here tonight and soon Nick will, too. I hope you don't want to keep this a secret."

"Pretty tough to do when I live on the square and people recognize your truck."

"Just checking." And good to know she didn't want to hide their relationship. That was a plus. Eventually they'd have to move beyond this private fantasy, but now that he had his foot in the door, he'd happily give her all the time she needed.

* * *

Fiona drifted off to sleep and he dozed a little, too. But he didn't allow himself to fall into a deep sleep. He took his job seriously and his decision to drive into town wasn't going to interfere with carrying out his duties at the ranch.

After ten years of waking early to begin the chores, his body clock was finely tuned to ranch rhythms. The room was still pitch black when he eased out of bed. Fiona didn't wake up.

He dressed quietly, listening for signs of the storm outside or Fiona stirring. Silence. Fiona slept and the storm was over. The electricity wasn't back on, though. He'd leave her the heavy-duty flashlight.

If he took off without waking her, she could get some undisturbed rest. But he needed his phone. And the drawer made a scratching sound.

No help for it, he'd have to open the drawer. When he did, the sheets rustled.

"Are you leaving?"

Her sleepy murmur stroked his nerve endings. If only he could crawl back into bed with her. "Yes." He took out his phone. "Sorry I woke you."

"I'm glad you did." More rustling. "I wouldn't have wanted you to go without telling me. Do you have two shovels in your truck?"

"Why?"

"I could help you dig out."

"That's generous, but I only have one." And he wouldn't let her do it no matter how many shovels he had in his truck.

"Wish I had one, but the town clears my walk so I never saw the need. Do you know if my robe's still on the floor?"

"I laid it across the end of the bed."

"Thanks. I can at least walk downstairs with you."

"Hey, I can manage the—"

"I'm sure you can since you have a flashlight on your phone. But I want to go down so I can listen by the door and make sure you can get out. Wait, you need that ginormous flashlight."

"I'm leaving that for you. My phone's charged but yours isn't."

"If you insist, but you can use it to see while you're shoveling and bring it back to me when you're done."

"I guess that makes sense."

"I'll get it." Her bare feet whispered across the floor and she opened the closet door. "What time is it?"

"Four-thirty."

"Yikes. That's early."

"Don't know how much snow I'll need to shovel."

"Do you have gloves?" Her footsteps moving in his direction sounded different. "I don't remember seeing—"

"I left them in the truck. Did you just put on slippers?"

"I did. See how perceptive you're getting?" She took his hand. "I have your flashlight. I'll lead the way downstairs."

"Okay." He wasn't going to stop her if it meant spending a little more time together. And the flashlight would help him get the truck out faster.

He counted steps to the stairway, though, for future reference. "Listen, I had an idea. You can nix it if you want."

"What?"

"You've never had a Christmas tree, right?"

"Never."

"What if I bring you a small one in a pot with just a few lights, maybe a couple of ornaments, and we set it in the corner of the bedroom?"

"That's a very romantic idea."

"I thought so."

"Would you want to keep the tree lights on during the night?"

"Up to you." But he hoped she would. It would be a start.

"Clever idea."

"What do you say?"

"I'd love a tree." She guided him toward the front door. Pale light filtered through the iced-over front windows. "The Moose's generators are still going."

The light allowed him to see her, but not well. "Can't risk spoiled food."

"That light should help you, too." She let go of his hand.

"Sure will." He located his boots and hat by the front door and put them on.

"I think I can risk unlocking the deadbolt. I don't hear the wind anymore."

He cocked his head. "But I do believe I hear snowplows."

"So do I, now that you mention it. I hope they've plowed the two-lane out to the ranch."

"There's a good chance they have." He stepped toward her. "I'll take that flashlight, now."

She handed it over. "You don't have to bring it back in. Even if the power isn't restored, I can manage until the sun comes up."

"What if I want to bring it back so I can kiss you goodbye?"

"Oh." There was a smile in her voice. "That's different."

"Move away. I'm going to open the door." He waited until she'd shifted to the side before giving it a tug. "Frozen shut." He put his back into it and the door came open with a loud crack. Cold air hit him in the face as he stepped into the snowdrift blocking the door.

Quickly pulling the door shut, he forged a path through the drift and out to the street. He was in luck. The wind had blown the snow toward the building. The sidewalk was impassable, but the street, at least the part behind his truck, was relatively clear.

The driver's side door was frozen shut, too, but it eventually gave way. Climbing into the frigid cab, he set the flashlight on the passenger seat as he coaxed the engine to life, sending clouds of smoke out the tailpipe.

He left the truck running while he trudged back through the snow with the flashlight. "Stand back, Fi." he called out. He hurried in and pushed the door closed.

She came toward him, a shadowy figure in her robe. Looked like the collar was turned up. "You can't be done already."

"Don't have to shovel. I'll just put it in reverse and I should be able to back right out of the drift."

"That's great."

He set down the flashlight by the door. "You might not want that kiss, after all. Just that short time out there and my jacket's—"

"I do want that kiss." She wasted no time moving in and wrapping her warm arms around his neck. "I can handle a little chill."

"Okay, then." He pulled her close. "Damn, you feel good. I'm going to miss you today."

"I'll miss you, too." She welcomed the press of his mouth, opening to him and inviting him to go deeper.

He couldn't resist. His tongue sought her familiar warmth and his body tightened in response. If he kept this up, he'd be hard and ready in two minutes.

With a frustrated moan, he lifted his head. "If I don't leave now, I'll—"

"Go." She wiggled out of his arms and gave him a little push. "Get out of here."

He sighed and reached for the door. "See you tonight. With the tree."

"If there's no wind, I'll leave the door unlocked."

"And you'll be waiting for me upstairs?"

"Uh-huh."

Fire licked at his privates. "See you then."

14

The power came on five minutes after Leo's truck pulled away. Fiona glanced around. Between the light spilling down the stairway and the security lights set into the baseboards of the shop, she would have come face-to-face with him.

And chances were excellent that the sexy, adventuresome lover she'd shown him tonight would have reverted to the tongue-tied, awestruck wimp he'd had dinner with at the Moose. She wasn't about to let that transformation happen.

She still couldn't see out any of her windows, but now that the heat was on the ice would start to melt and the sun would finish the job. Snowplows rumbled down her street, scraping snow from the pavement. Soon the work crews would be out shoveling the walkways.

Looked like businesses would be open, including hers. Normally everything closed on Sundays, but the town council had recently relaxed the rules for Christmas week.

She'd be open from ten to five today. And she'd be meeting Beth and Eva for coffee at Cup of Cheer at twelve-thirty so they could hear about Operation Santa.

Eva had the day off at Tres Beau Salon, but Beth and Fiona couldn't afford more than a thirty-minute break this time of year. They'd agreed to eat their usual quick lunch at their respective shops first. But thirty minutes at Cup of Cheer wouldn't be nearly enough considering the news she had to share.

Climbing the stairs to her apartment, she walked into her bedroom and turned on the horseshoe lamp. She'd never look at it the same way again.

Or the bed, or the sheets. She stripped them off and breathed in the heady aroma of hot sex and citrus cologne. Her core clenched. Oh, yeah, she wanted to hold onto this fantasy as long as possible.

Tossing the sheets in the washer, she headed for the shower. It would be another two-shower day and that was fine with her. Oh. Her phone. She walked through her apartment naked, something she'd never done before, to retrieve it.

She charged it in the bathroom so she could play Mannheim Steamroller while she showered and washed her hair. She'd never listen to their music the same way again, either.

Technically she should be tired. Instead, energy flowed through her and she hummed along with the music. He would be back tonight. *Tonight.*

Was this how life had been for Winifred Barton when she'd received nightly visits from her secret lover? But Leo wasn't a secret. No doubt their relationship would be common knowledge at the Buckskin Ranch by the end of the day. From there the news would spread to the Babes, who watched over the men of the Brotherhood like proud aunties.

But a rendezvous in the dark added mystery and an extra dose of erotic pleasure. Reading Miss Barton's journal had opened Fiona's eyes to the possibilities for spicing up an affair. Audacious outfits made no sense in the dark, but that saucy lady had hinted at various other ways she'd tantalized her lover. Racy Lace had some of those items.

As she was drying off and singing along to *Carol of the Bells*, Leo's text came through. She grabbed the phone eagerly.

Made it back safely. Miss you already. Nick said Eva's having coffee with you and Beth. Will you tell them?

She texted right back. *Yes. I'll ask Beth if she has anything interesting that we could have fun with. Would you like that?*

You're torturing me.

She sent him a smiley face. Then a face blowing a kiss.

My phone doesn't have emojis for what I'm thinking.

Her skin flushed. *Mine, either. See you at 8. Count on it.*

The text exchange powered her through her morning routine and a flood of last-minute Christmas shoppers. She ate a quick lunch of tomato soup and crackers. At twenty-five minutes past noon, she hung her *Will Return* clock face sign on her window and set the hands for one.

Bundling up in a coat, scarf, hat, gloves and snow boots, she cut diagonally across the square toward Cup of Cheer on the opposite corner. The untrammeled snow from early morning was now a series of footpaths. A snowman sat in a cleared space near the gazebo.

Halfway there, Beth called out for her to wait. Fiona paused as her friend hurried across the snow, her cheeks rosy from the cold.

"How was it?" Beth tugged her furry hat over her ears. "Did you have a good time?"

"Obviously you haven't talked to Eva."

"No." She frowned. "Did something go wrong?"

Fiona laughed. "Something went right. Very, very right. I'll tell you when we get there."

"Wow, I can't wait to hear. Did Clark Smith turn out to be a fun guy?"

"You could say that." She waved to Eva, who stood by the front door of the coffee shop. "Hey, go grab us a table!"

Eva gave her a thumbs-up and ducked inside. She was holding down a spot by the window when they came in. "Just get me a peppermint cappuccino. I'll hold our spot."

Fiona nodded. "Will do."

Eva pulled off the stocking cap, revealing her trademark blue hair, and flashed her a big smile. "Way to go, by the way."

"Way to go?" Beth stuffed her gloves in her pocket. "What happened last night?"

"Why don't you give me your order, too? That way you can get the info from Eva."

Beth dug in her wallet. "I'll have what Eva's having."

"Put your money away. I'm in a buying mood."

"Okay, then." Beth's gray eyes gleamed with interest. "See you in a bit." She hurried over to join Eva.

A minute later a loud *oh, my God* made Fiona smile. Giggles and low murmurs followed. She glanced over her shoulder and gave them a wave. Wearing huge grins, they waved back.

She turned toward the counter as the couple in front of her finished their order and moved over to the pickup window. "Oh, my goodness!" She smiled at Isabel, the shop's owner, who was due to deliver her baby girl any day. "I didn't expect to see you here."

Isabel returned her smile. "I'd rather be at the shop accomplishing something than hanging around the house waiting for Cleo Marie to show up."

"Makes sense. How are you feeling?"

"Large. Very large. What can I get for you?"

"Three peppermint cappuccinos, please."

Isabel relayed the order and rang it up. "Henri's already written in the journal Ben got at your shop yesterday."

"She has?" She handed Isabel cash and took her change.

"She took a picture of her first entry and texted it to me. Dear Cleo Marie, Get the lead out, girl. I'm chewing nails waiting for you. Buckets of love, Gramma Henri."

Fiona laughed. "What fun."

"And what a loving thing to do. She's my rock. My parents should have been here by now, but all flights out of SeaTac are grounded by a massive storm."

"Aww, I'm sorry."

"They'll make it eventually, but in the meantime, I have the Buckskin gang and the Babes."

"And CJ."

Isabel chuckled. "Poor guy's a nervous wreck. Good thing he has the Brotherhood."

"Yep, they're awesome." *Especially Leo.* She glanced at the pickup counter. "Looks like my order's up. I hope Cleo Marie makes her entrance soon."

"Thanks. Me, too."

Fiona put the three steaming mugs on a tray and carried them to the table. Her friends had their heads together, clearly enjoying a conversation they didn't want overheard. They both glanced up when she arrived.

"What a story, Fi," Beth said. "I should have known there was something fishy when Ben handed the job to somebody we've never heard of."

"I knew the plan from the get-go." Eva looked smug. "Nick told me all about it when he came home from the wrapping party at the Moose. But I wasn't allowed to tell."

"I'm glad you didn't." Fiona passed out the drinks and pulled up a chair. "That would have ruined it, and he did an amazing job maintaining the disguise. I didn't guess until he took off the hat and the beard."

"But are you going to keep him literally in the dark?" Eva wrapped her hands around her mug. "Nick told me that was the agreement, but—"

"I don't see how you can keep that up."
Beth leaned forward and lowered her voice. "Men
are visual creatures, if you know what I mean."

"He says he's okay with it, and when I can't
see him, I'm..." She dropped her voice, too. "I've
never been this uninhibited with a man. It really
works for me."

Eva nodded. "Then stick to the program. At
least for the time being."

"I plan to. I feel like I'm channeling
Winifred Barton, in a way, although sexy nightwear
makes no sense in the dark." She turned to Beth.
"I'd like to check out some of your other fun stuff,
maybe tonight after you close."

"Absolutely. We'll make a private party of
it."

"What a great idea, Fi," Eva said. "Would it
be okay if I came over, too?"

"I'd love having both of you there. I've
never tried to be a temptress before. I could use
some advice."

"You must be doing a decent job so far.
Nick says Leo's on cloud nine today."

"So am I." Her cheeks heated. "I can't stop
thinking about him."

Beth's forehead puckered. "Do you picture
his face? Because I would think—"

"I don't picture his face."

Her friends cracked up.

"Hey, I didn't mean it that way. I think
about... well, okay, maybe I do think about what
you think I'm thinking about."

Beth wiped tears from her cheeks. "I think
you're going to be our entertainment for the

holidays, Fi. I'm so looking forward to watching how this unfolds."

"That makes two of us." Eva leaned forward and lowered her voice. "Listen, slight change of subject. Adele, the funeral director, came in for her hair appointment this morning and we got to talking about Winifred. I might have a clue about her secret lover."

Fiona sucked in a breath. "Awesome."

"Last Christmas Day, someone put a holiday wreath on Winifred's grave. Adele spotted it on the twenty-sixth when she went back to work."

"Sounds like a clue to me," Beth said. "The last entry in her journal was on Christmas Day."

"I thought of that, too." Eva gazed at her. "In my mind, that Christmas was the end of their affair. Unless she just got sick of keeping the journal."

"I think we all know that's unlikely." Excitement tightened Fiona's chest. "I'll bet he's still alive. That was the first Christmas after she died. What if he does it again this year?"

"That's what Adele wondered." Eva took a sip of her coffee. "But since she has no idea about the journal or the secret lover, it's just idle curiosity on her part and she's not going to stake out the gravesite on Christmas."

"But I might."

"Are you kidding, Fi?" Eva's eyes widened. "You'd spend Christmas in a graveyard?"

"Only a tiny bit of it. Assuming this is her secret lover, he doesn't want to be seen and he's elderly so he might not like to drive at night. That leaves dawn and dusk. I could go over at sundown. If he's been there, I'll know to arrive before dawn next year. If there's no wreath, I'll wait to see if he shows up.'"

"Good thinking," Eva said. "Since they were evening lovers, my bet would be dusk."

"Makes sense," Beth said. "I'd go with you, except Jared and I are—"

"I wouldn't dream of interfering with your Christmas plans. I'll handle this."

"I'll be having dinner with Nick and the rest of the Buckskin gang." Eva held her gaze. "Now that you're with Leo, you'll probably be invited."

"I didn't think of that." She shoved down an attack of nerves. "I'll burn that bridge when I come to it. But I plan to be at the cemetery at twilight."

Beth finished off her cappuccino. "What if he shows up? Will you talk to him?"

"I don't want to intrude on his private moment, but once I know who he is, I think we should give him the journal at some point."

"You should be the one to give it to him," Eva said. "You've done all the digging into back issues of the *Gazette*."

"I agree." Beth nodded. "Besides, he might be embarrassed that someone's been privy to those intimate moments he shared with Winifred. You don't have to tell him all three of us read the journal."

"No reason to. My idea was to approach him between Christmas and New Year's."

Beth looked at her. "You think you know who it is, don't you?"

"Yes, but I might be on the wrong track. And the person who left the wreath could be one of her women friends who remembers how she used to decorate that beautiful Victorian for the holidays."

"She sure did." Eva's face lit up. "I was going to surprise you guys but I can't stand the suspense. When you come over on the twenty-third, you'll be treated to so many vintage decorations. They were stored in three of the boxes Nick lugged down from the attic."

"Oh, right, we're getting together on the twenty-third." Leo had driven that event right out of her head.

Beth smiled. "Think you can make it? Or will you be otherwise occupied?"

"I can make it. I just—"

"Don't worry, Fi. We'll wrap up early." Eva gave her a wink.

"Look, I don't want you to change the plans for me."

"Why not? The Brotherhood's having their traditional guys-only celebration at the bunkhouse that night, but these days, they're all eager to get back to the women in their lives. That includes Leo."

15

The first major blizzard of the winter meant snow removal by tractor and shovel was the order of the day at the Buckskin. Leo relished the hard labor. It didn't keep him from missing Fiona, but it relieved the tension missing her produced.

The long day ended with a cherished tradition—a snowball fight in the meadow behind the fire pit. The teams had been established years ago—Matt, Jake and Rafe, aka the Cow Patties, versus CJ, Nick and Leo, the Horse Apples. Seth had been the somewhat impartial referee for snowball fights, and like most referees, he'd taken a fair share of abuse.

Garrett had volunteered to handle the job, but Leo had his doubts that kind, soft-spoken Garrett could deal with it. He'd kept his opinion to himself as Garrett reviewed the rules with Matt, captain of the Cow Patties, and CJ, captain of the Horse Apples.

When they returned to their respective bunkers, Leo took Garrett aside. "You don't have to do it. You can have my spot on the Horse Apples and I'll referee."

Garrett smiled. "But I want to referee." He'd weather-proofed his Stetson and tied it on with a length of rawhide, copying everyone else's method of protection.

"Just warning you. We'll question your calls. We gave Seth all kinds of grief. But he was used to it. You—"

"I was Seth's replacement so it makes sense for me to take over this job."

Matt leaned on the shovel he was using to heap more snow on his team's bunker. "Hey, Leo, no bribing the ref."

"Just letting him know what he's in for. I offered to take it, instead."

Matt nodded. "Noble of you, Leo. But seeing as how I have seniority, if anybody is taking over for Garrett, it'll be me. If you'd rather be a Cow Patty, buddy, I'll ref."

"Hey!" CJ called over. "Nice try, Matt. The Cow Patty captain making the calls? I think not. You—"

"I'm taking the job." Garrett raised his hand and silver flashed in the fading sunlight. "I have possession of Seth's whistle and I know how to use it."

"Alrighty, then." CJ went back to stockpiling ammunition. "Better get to work, Matt. It's gonna take a lot of balls to win this thing."

"Big balls, baby-daddy," Jake called over. "And we've got 'em."

"We start in one minute!" Garrett's shout projected authority.

Impressive shout. Leo had never heard Garrett raise his voice. Maybe he had the moxie to take command, after all.

"Players, take your positions!"

Leo crouched behind the four-foot mound of snow they'd created and glanced at Nick. "Didn't know he could sound like a drill sergeant."

"I'm guessing there's plenty we don't know about Garrett. Matt wants to initiate him into the Brotherhood tomorrow night."

"Yeah?"

"He thinks we should bring him in before Cleo Marie is born, so he can be an official uncle, too."

"I vote yes."

"Good. I'll tell Matt."

"On my mark. Three, two, *one*." Garrett blasted the whistle.

Ears ringing from the whistle and the yelling, Leo grabbed snowball after snowball, firing them across the clearing as heads popped up behind the Cow Patty fort.

Garrett kept score better than Seth had, calling the points for direct hits, adding them up as he went. When he took guff, he didn't argue back. Instead he stopped the action and blew the whistle continuously until the complaining party laughed and gave up.

"Cow Patties twelve, Horse Apples eight!"

Jake rose to his feet, left arm mounded with snowballs, right arm cocked. "Kamikaze! Cow Patties, cover me!"

Rounding the bunker, he raced forward, firing as he went, taking snowballs in the face and chest but using his higher position to score more points than he lost.

Leo loaded up and jumped to his feet. "Kamikaze! Horse Apples, cover me!"

"Can't, bro!" CJ shouted back. "Jake's got us blocked!"

Suicide mission time. "*Dances with Wolves!*" Ditching his snowballs, he extended his arms like Kevin Costner in the opening scene of the movie and managed to catch most of the ones coming his way. Whenever he shot them back, he got double points.

A yell from CJ signaled that Jake had breached the Horse Apple fortress. Racing forward, Leo threw himself spread-eagled on the Cow Patty bunker, crushing it under his weight as Garrett's whistle screeched.

As soon as everyone was upright and had wiped the snow from their faces, the Brotherhood converged on Garrett.

Jake took the lead. "Cow Patties won, right?"

Garrett shook his head.

"Horse Apples rule!" Nick punched a fist in the air.

Garrett shook his head again. "It was a draw."

"That can't be right." Leo brushed off his coat. "I was a snowball-catching machine out there."

"You were good, but so was Jake." Garrett regarded them calmly. "It's a draw."

"Can't be," CJ said. "The Horse Apples have to maintain their streak."

Garrett folded his arms. "How long is this streak?"

"Just one win, but still, we—"

"It's a draw." Garrett stared him down.

Jake shook the snow from his hat. "So we're buying our own drinks at the Moose on Christmas Eve?"

"That's one way to look at it," Garrett said. "The other way is to be glad you're not buying drinks for the Horse Apples."

"Ha!" Nick pointed a finger at Jake. "And we're not buying drinks for the Cow Patties, either."

Garrett smiled. "Win-win."

"Speaking of drinks," Rafe said, "who's ready for one? I might not agree with the verdict, but let's hash it out over bottles of brew."

"Great idea, teammate." Jake clapped him on the shoulder.

As they all headed back to the bunkhouse, Leo fell into step beside Garrett. He lowered his voice. "Was it really a draw?"

Garrett chuckled. "Couldn't tell you. I lost count during that kamikaze, *Dances with Wolves* thing you guys did. Next time I'll be prepared. Might bring a counter for each hand."

"We don't always do those moves."

"You don't?"

"Sometimes we do other stuff."

"So I'll learn on the job. What's life without a challenge?"

"Charley used to say that a lot." Which emphasized why Garrett would be a worthy member of the Brotherhood.

He'd be the first to be welcomed into the group since it was formed. Did Matt have an initiation ceremony in mind? And how long would it run?

The second he asked himself that question, guilt pricked him hard. The ceremony would take as long as it needed to. If it cut into his time with Fiona, that was the breaks. The Brotherhood took priority.

* * *

The roads were clear, which made calculating the time needed to arrive at Fiona's easy. He added a couple extra minutes to pick up the tree. She'd said eight, and he didn't want to show up early. Or late.

He'd called the nursery earlier in the day. Good thing the place had Sunday hours this week. The owner had agreed to sell him a display model, a decorated two-footer in a fancy pot. It would be waiting by the nursery gate since the place closed at five.

He spotted it immediately when he pulled up to the curb. His high beams picked up colorful ornaments, red bows and a glittering star on top. Even without the lights on, it looked festive.

He didn't trust putting it in the truck bed, so he carefully tucked it on the floor of the back seat. It made the cab smell like Christmas. Now that he'd experienced the holidays at the Buckskin, he couldn't imagine going without the fresh pine scent of a tree.

He'd asked the nursery to include a waterproof saucer to put under the pot. Those original hardwood floors didn't need to be ruined by water stains. And he didn't want the lights to ruin the ambiance she treasured.

If the door was unlocked, he could find a plug and test the lights before taking it up there. If they were too bright, he wouldn't suggest turning them on. Not tonight, anyway.

His heartbeat ramped up as he parked in front of Planet-Friendly Paper. The shop was dimly lit the way it had been last night before the blackout—security lights on plus the glow from the square filtering in.

But her apartment was completely dark. His groin tightened. She was waiting for him, likely naked, in her bed.

A small part of him chafed against this light restriction, but it had a certain appeal, too. In the dark, anything could happen. She'd spent time shopping at Racy Lace for items to surprise and tease him. She planned to seduce him and he was ready to be seduced.

Pocketing his keys and his phone, he maneuvered the tree out of the back seat and picked up the saucer underneath. He needed to test the lights on the tree. Ignoring the persistent ache from his package, he reached for the door handle. Open.

He slipped inside with the tree, closed the door and flipped the deadbolt. He'd tracked in some slush, so he took his boots off and left them by the door. Might as well prop his hat on top of them like he had before.

She'd have plugs near the cash register so he headed in that direction, pulled out his phone and turned on the flashlight. There. A power strip with a vacant spot.

He unwound the cord from the base of the pot, set the tree on the floor and crouched down to plug it in. Nice. Small, multi-colored lights created a soft glow. Maybe she wouldn't mind the—

"Oh, my goodness, that's so pretty!"

He stood, doused the flashlight app and turned, partially blocking the light and putting himself in shadow. The ambient glow touched her golden hair and revealed the color of her soft robe—Christmas red. "Not too bright?"

"No." Her voice softened as she moved toward him, bringing with her a tantalizing scent.

"You're wearing a different perfume."

"It's called *Tempting Fate*."

"It's tempting the heck out of me." Did she just untie her sash?

"That's the idea. The tree's lovely. Thank you for bringing it."

His breath caught as her robe parted. Her breasts, illuminated by the tree, quivered with each breath as she approached. Her bare feet made almost no noise. Taking a step forward, he reached for her.

"I heard you open the door, but when you didn't come upstairs—"

"I was testing the tree." His voice sounded like boots on gravel. Sliding his hands inside her robe, he pulled her close and groaned. She was on fire.

"It's beautiful."

"So are you." He kissed her and lost his mind.

16

Fiona had scripted a different start to the evening, but once Leo's ravenous mouth captured hers, she abandoned her plan and went with his. It involved a lot of kissing, fondling, and getting him out of his jacket.

During their uneven progress to the stairs, his jacket landed on the floor, giving her access to the snaps down the front of his shirt. At the foot of the staircase, he plunged his tongue into her mouth, cupped her bottom in both hands and pressed her aching cleft against the straining denim of his fly.

If that was an invitation, she was taking it. He'd skipped wearing a belt again. Smart man. She unfastened the button on his jeans and reached for the tab on his zipper.

He lifted his head, gasping. "If you... open that—"

"What?"

"We'll never... make it... to your bedroom."

"Don't care." She gulped as she struggled with the zipper. "Back off a bit."

Shifting his hips so she could open his fly, he dragged in a breath. "Ever done it on the stairs?"

"Nope."

"You're about to." Edging them to the foot of the steps, he lifted her up and settled her above him. "Hold onto—" He cleared his throat and dug in his pocket. "My shoulders."

She gripped hard, needing the solid feel of his muscular body to keep from shaking herself right off her perch. At least her bathrobe would keep her from getting splinters in her tush. Never in a million years would she have—

"Lean back." He swallowed. "I've got you."

Supported by his arm and holding onto his shoulders for dear life, she did as he asked. Using his other arm for balance, he knelt on the step below her and moved between her thighs. "Ah, Fiona." With a low moan of relief, he firmly claimed his place inside her quivering body.

Her core muscles clenched and she dug her fingers into his shoulders. "Missed you."

"I can tell." His voice was strained. "Nice welcome."

"Thought about this... all day."

"Me, too." His cock twitched.

"Didn't expect stair sex."

His chuckle sounded breathless. "Nobody would. You okay?"

"Never better. Gonna move?"

"Yes, ma'am." He eased back and pushed deep.

Her stair creaked. "This one—"

"Let's make some music." He stroked slowly at first, then picked up the pace.

The wooden step responded with a rhythmic chirp that made her giggle. But soon her laughter became incoherent cries. Planting her bare feet on the smooth wood, she gave herself up to his sweet assault as he coaxed her to the brink and hurled her into a whirlpool of glorious release.

Swearing softly, he shoved home one more time and came, his body shuddering as he pinned her to the stairway. Anchored by the instrument of her pleasure, she wrapped him in her arms. His shirt clung to his sweaty body and she clung to him. If she never had to move, that would be okay.

Moments later, his warm breath tickled her ear. "You were wonderful."

"You, too. It's a fun idea." She arched her neck as he nuzzled her there. "Great first experience for me."

"For me, too."

"You've never done this before?"

"No, ma'am. But, I figured we could handle it."

"You acted like you were an old hand."

"I acted like a man who couldn't wait another second to be deep inside you."

She smiled. "Must have been my new perfume."

"Oh, it was a factor, but when you walked toward me with your robe undone, I was toast, with or without the new perfume."

"I'm not sure what came over me. I just... wanted to do that and see what happened."

"This happened."

"I'm not sorry. Don't you think the creaking stair made it sexier?"

"Definitely. Especially when it was added to the hoarse cries of a woman enjoying the heck out of coming."

"I did enjoy the heck out of it."

"So did I. But we have to move."

"Don't wanna."

"Got to. Will I have to climb the stairs to take care of—"

"There's a bathroom down here."

"Good. Directions, please."

"The door's under this stairway."

"I think I can find that." He eased away from her and stood. "Wait here, please."

"No, thank you. I'm going upstairs."

"Without me?"

"Exactly." She pulled her robe together. "I loved this detour we just took, but now I can proceed with my original plan. I'll be waiting for you in my bedroom. Want me to take the tree upstairs?"

He laughed. "I'd like to do that."

"Then I'll see you soon." She caught herself. "I mean—"

"I know what you mean." His tone was gentle. "I'll be up there in a couple of minutes."

"Okay." She grabbed the railing and pulled herself up. An epic orgasm could leave a girl a little weak in the knees. *Any* contact with Leo Marston could leave a girl weak in the knees.

Then again, she'd brought *him* to his knees, literally. He'd been so overcome he'd made love to her on the stairs. The perfume Beth had recommended probably helped, but that sexy walk with her robe hanging open had likely clinched the deal.

When he'd turned with his back to the light, he'd set up the perfect scenario. He was a faceless silhouette but hadn't blocked all the light from the tree. Any that had bypassed his broad shoulders and wide chest had landed on her.

She'd been able to give him the visual stimulation Beth said was the nuclear option with guys. She insisted the sight of their lover's body aroused them more than anything else. Evidently so. Couldn't argue with Leo's response to it.

Taking a deep breath, she hurried up the stairs. They'd need some snuggling time to recover from stair sex, but then… she was eager to try out one or two of her purchases.

She wouldn't blow through her entire stash, though. Beth had taught her that making love in the dark wasn't a man's natural preference. They enjoyed light and plenty of it.

Thanks to Beth's helpful consultation this afternoon, she understood the male psyche better than she ever had. She was working against Leo's inclinations, which meant she had to keep sessions in the dark interesting if she wanted to make this adventure last a while.

Slipping out of her robe, she hung it on a hook on the back of her bedroom door and climbed into bed

The creaky step announced that Leo was on his way. Her security lights in the shop plus a glow from the square would allow him to see his path up the stairs far better than he had the night before. After that he'd be surrounded by darkness.

She called out to him. "Need any help finding your way?"

"Thanks. I've got it."

His muted footsteps and the scent of fresh pine signaled he was almost to her door. "Where do you want the tree?"

"In the left corner, please. Think you can find it?"

"I know I can. I have a map in my head. Hazards noted."

"FYI, I took the horseshoe lamp out of here."

He chuckled. "Appreciate it. When I'm going for a condom, I could forget all about that thing."

"The tree smells terrific." It blended nicely with his cologne.

"Sure does." The rhythm of his breathing and the movement of air indicated he was passing by the end of the bed.

She shivered with excitement. The stairway adventure had been fun, but she preferred naked, skin-to-skin contact. It was only moments away.

"I brought a waterproof saucer to put under the pot." Rustling noises followed as he set it down in the corner and positioned the pot inside it.

"Good idea. There's a plug on the window wall." And she'd just had a good idea of her own.

"Close your eyes. I'm using my phone flashlight to find the plug."

"That's fine." She closed her eyes and waited, pulse racing.

"Found the plug. Ready for me to turn it on?"

"Ready." She rolled to her side facing the tree and Leo.

The jewel-toned lights winked on, soft and atmospheric. Crouching in front of it, he straightened the star on top. "What do you think?"

"Very nice." His movements stretched his dark-toned shirt, pulling it taut across his muscular back. He hadn't worn one of his ugly ones this time. Silver piping outlined the yoke, emphasizing his broad shoulders.

"Want me to leave it on?"

She swallowed. "Yes, please."

"I'm glad." He stood and slowly turned in her direction, his face in shadow. "Because I really like—" He froze.

His sharp inhale was exactly what she'd been going for. "You didn't finish your thought." She stroked her hand over her hip and took a deep breath, expanding her chest. "What is it that you really like, cowboy?"

17

Leo drank in the longed-for sight of Fiona stretched out naked on the bed, her golden hair spilling over her shoulder in soft waves and curling against her ivory skin. He looked his fill, his heartbeat thudding in his ears as it pumped his blood south.

She blushed, adding sparkle to her green eyes. The blush spread to her plump breasts, which quivered when she took another breath. As her nipples puckered, saliva pooled in his mouth. He swallowed. "You're incredible."

"I love it when you get that rough note in your voice."

"It's a wonder I can speak." His fingers trembled as he finished undoing the snaps on his shirt. "I didn't think… you said you wanted…"

"Darkness. I know. I feel bold and daring in the dark."

"Then why…" His brain stalled as she cupped her breast and toyed with her nipple.

"Because I just found out how much you like the light."

"I sure do." He stripped off his shirt, dropped it on the floor and reached for the button on his jeans.

"I think I stunned you a little bit just now."

"Yes, ma'am." He fumbled with his zipper. "I'm shaking, Fi."

"Want some help?"

"I want you." He wrestled the zipper down, grabbed a condom from his pocket and put it between his teeth so he could shove his jeans and briefs to the floor. Stepping out of them, he made quick work of putting on the condom.

Damn, he was breathing like a freight train. And ready to come. Even after the episode on the stairs, he was frantic to bury himself in her hot body. He put a knee on the bed and she moved over to make room. "I feel like..." He paused to suck in air. "A sex-starved teenager."

"Is that good or bad?"

"Depends on whether you mind that I want you again."

"I don't mind at all."

"That's good news." Moving between her thighs and bracing himself on his forearms, he watched her eyes as he pushed slowly into her slick channel. Poised over her, he cast a shadow, but not enough to rob him of the view of her bright gaze. "Can you see me?"

"Not well." She cupped his face and coaxed him down to her waiting mouth. "And that allows me to focus on this."

He closed his eyes and claimed her mouth as he sank deeper. She didn't want eye contact. Not yet. But he could wait.

And in the meantime….

Once he was locked in tight, he remained still, concentrating on kissing her for the few seconds it took for him to resist the urge to climax. When he could move again, he eased up a little and slowly rotated his hips.

"Mmm."

He lifted his mouth from hers. "Like that?"

"Uh-huh."

He did it again and she quivered beneath him. Pulling back, he combined a deep thrust with a hip rotation.

She gasped. "More of that."

"You bet." Pleasing her was such a joy. He sped things up and she urged him on, panting and crying out as her core tightened. And tightened some more.

Shifting her grip from his face to his glutes, she held on tight as he went faster yet, his breathing ragged, his body begging for release.

"*There!*" Her fingers dug in and her orgasm rolled over his rigid cock.

He rocked into her once more, wringing breathless cries from her lips. Then, with a shout that emptied his lungs, he bowed to the demands of his testosterone-fueled body. The force of his climax sent shock waves from the soles of his feet to the roots of his hair. His ears rang and his body shook. Maybe he was having a heart attack.

That would be okay. He rested his forehead against her shoulder and fought for breath. He could think of worse ways to die than while he was making explosive love to Fiona Hildebrand.

* * *

As it turned out, he recovered. Gradually the world stopped spinning and he could breathe again. Lifting his head, he gazed down at her. He couldn't tell for sure because even with the tree on, the shadows ruled. But he thought she looked happy. "Are you smiling?"

"I am. I think it's a permanent condition."

"My ears are still ringing."

"Mine, too. That rotation move of yours was way more fun than I expected. Can we try it again, sometime?"

"I'm game. Even if I did think that climax was gonna kill me."

"Mine was pretty intense, too." She chuckled. "Not sure my heart can take it, but what a way to go."

"Agreed." He gave her a quick kiss. "Be right back." The light from the Christmas tree helped him some as he headed for the door. He counted steps to her bathroom and turned on the light, since he was in there by himself.

As he was washing up, he caught sight of the dazed, smiling dude in the mirror, the guy who looked like he was one bottle shy of a six-pack. He laughed as he finished up and shut off the light. Fiona drove him crazy, and he couldn't wait to climb back into her bed so she could do it some more.

The tree only lit the far corner, which allowed him to see the shadow of the bed, but not where she'd positioned herself. "Where do you want me?"

"In bed. Snuggled close."

His cock twitched. He sent it a signal to stand down. At least for the time being. "Which side?"

"On the tree side, please."

He walked around the foot of the bed. "Are you going to flash me again? Because if you are, I'll just go straight to my jeans pocket and grab another raincoat."

"I'm not going to flash you. That would be repetitious."

"Not in my book. That routine never gets old."

"I'll keep that in mind."

He had a better view on the far side of the bed. She'd pulled the sheet and comforter up to her chin, which was sexy in its own way since she was naked under those covers. She'd left him a generous portion of the bed. Too generous. He'd fix that.

"I gave you the warm spot."

"Thoughtful." He got in and reached for her. "Let's share it."

"I'd like that." She snuggled close and something furry slid up his chest.

He yelped and rolled away, nearly falling out of bed. "What the hell?"

She started laughing. "It's a mitten."

"It's not alive?"

"It's a fake fur mitten. Sorry, I should have warned you."

He turned back toward her. "I thought it was a ferret."

She got the giggles. "Do you often end up in bed with a ferret?"

"No! But I knew a woman who had one. Its coat felt like that. Why are you wearing a mitten?"

"Sensual stimulation."

"Something from Beth's shop?"

"Yes. Want me to do it again, now that you know it's not a ferret?"

"I guess so."

She stroked his chest. "How does that feel?"

"Furry. I'm not used to having something furry against my skin. Manly men don't—"

"Do you like it?"

"Depends on whether that will be our little secret."

"It will." She moved from his chest to his waist and around to his back. "No one has to know but me that you're practically purring."

"Am not."

"You just went *mmmm* like a big jungle cat would sound purring."

"Do I get to use it on you?"

"Eventually. But it's my turn, now." She scooted back. "Lie on your stomach so I can have a bigger surface to work on."

He rolled over and she lightly massaged his back before shoving down the covers and using the mitten on his glutes and thighs. He shivered.

"Are you cold?"

"No."

"Aroused?"

"Not exactly. Just... sensitized, electrified, like I could shoot sparks out of my fingertips."

"Cool."

"But this could lead to something."

"Think so?"

"Yes, ma'am, and I promised myself we'd take a break."

"We're taking one now."

"The way my nerves are tingling, it won't be a long break. I—" A familiar melody floated up from the floor near the Christmas tree where he'd left his phone.

She stopped stroking him. "Is *Lord of the Rings* your sister?"

"Yep." He turned over and sat up. "She probably opened her present."

"Answer it," she said gently. "Please."

_18_

When Leo left the bed to grab his phone, Fiona slid out on the other side, crossed to the door and unhooked her bathrobe. His cheerful voice when he answered the phone made her glad she'd coaxed him to pick up. Putting on the robe, she walked into her darkened living room.

She couldn't hear what he was saying, but his easy laughter and warm tone told her everything she needed to know about his love for his sister. And that he missed her. What was the story there?

Belting the robe, she continued into her kitchen to get a drink of water. Maybe Leo would like one, too. After all that exercise. She smiled. Or maybe she could come up with something more inspired than water.

She had spiced apple cider in her fridge. If she warmed it up, they could have part of the treat they'd missed the night before. When he got off the phone, she'd offer him that. He was, after all, a guest in her home.

Might as well take the cider out of the fridge and pour it into a pan, just in case. She turned on the light over the stove to give her a little more illumination.

As she poured the cider into the pan, Leo's voice became more distinct. She turned as his shadowy form emerged from her bedroom.

"Yep, she's read all the books and seen all the movies."

He was talking about *her*?

"Hang on, I'll see." He stayed in the bedroom doorway, backlit by the Christmas tree glow. He'd put on his jeans and shirt, although it hung loose, probably open.

He pressed the phone to his chest and lowered his voice. "Penny would like to say hi. Are you okay with that?"

"Are you?"

"Absolutely. She always asks if I'm seeing anybody, and for a change I was happy to say that I was. Will you talk to her?"

She was confused by the request, but touched that he'd ask. "Sure. I was about to warm up some cider. Want some?"

"Sounds good. Is it in that pan on the stove?"

"Yep."

"Then let me take care of that while you talk to Penny." He handed her his phone and headed for her kitchen.

His broad back and narrow hips were becoming a familiar and heart-stirring silhouette. She put the phone to her ear. "Hi, Penny. This is Fiona."

"Hey, there, Fiona! I can't believe my cowboy brother found a *Lord of the Rings* fan. That's awesome!"

"He told me you were really into it." She kept her eye on Leo as he surveyed her kitchen. He had enough light from the stove to get the layout.

"I have been into *LOTR* since I was a kid."

"Me, too." She watched Leo study the knobs on the stove before switching one on. Then he stepped back, shoving his hands in his pockets.

"I'll bet you were Galadriel for Halloween."

"Several times." When Leo turned to face her, she tensed, but his features were still in shadow. The dim light only let her see his silhouette.

"Did he tell you what he got me for Christmas?"

"No."

"Hobbit feet slippers and a shower curtain with a scene from the Shire."

"Nice."

"I'm a total geek, so I love them. I wasn't supposed to open the package, but I couldn't wait. Then I had to call to thank him, and to my surprise, I discovered that he was dating you. I thought he'd given up on finding someone."

"Evidently not." But she might not be that someone, not if she slid back into mouse mode when she finally saw him in the light. That would suck, but she wasn't kidding herself that she'd licked that problem. Her flinch when he'd turned to face her confirmed that.

"He's had terrible luck with women. They're all about his looks, which are admittedly amazing, but he hates it when people focus on that aspect. He said you're different."

"I guess that's true."

"If you're into *Lord of the Rings*, that's absolutely true. He said you own a shop called Planet-Friendly Paper. Right up my alley."

"You're an environmentalist?"

"Sure am. But I love journaling in longhand so I search out the kinds of notebooks you carry. Listen, I don't want to interrupt your evening any more than I already have. But it's been great talking to you. Merry Christmas."

"Same to you. I'll give you back to Leo." She held out the phone.

He walked toward her, took it and put it to his ear. "Hey, sis. Yeah, she's special. So what are you doing for your Christmas break?"

Fiona walked over to check on the cider. Switching off the heat, she took mugs out of the cupboard.

"Sounds like fun." He paused. "Haven't opened mine yet. I'm not like you. I wait. Merry Christmas, sis. Talk soon."

Steam rose from the cider pan. She poured it into the mugs, switched off the stove light and turned around as Leo came toward her.

Talking to his sister had unnerved her. She'd temporarily compartmentalized this affair as an adventure out of time. Her conversation with Penny didn't fit that scenario.

Leo wrapped his arms around her waist. "Thank you for talking to Penny. She worries about me."

"Because she loves you." She rested her hands on his bare chest. "Guess you decided not to have your conversation while you were naked."

"She's my little sister. Didn't seem right."

"You mentioned a Christmas break. Is she in school?"

"She teaches English Lit at UCLA." Capturing her hands, he placed them around his neck, bringing her closer.

"Has she ever been here?"

"Not yet. Maybe this summer." He drew her into his arms. "She was fifteen when I left and for several years she was mad at me for taking off. Mom and Dad convinced her I was a selfish SOB."

She nestled closer, laying her cheek against his warm skin. "I'm sorry."

"It's okay." He rubbed her back. "We're good now. She's been super-busy fast-tracking her career. Got her doctorate in June."

"Impressive."

"Yep. I would've gone to her graduation, but the folks still hate my guts, so me showing up could have ruined her big day."

"That sucks, Leo." Her parents weren't very demonstrative, but they loved her.

"I've made peace with it. So has Penny. Like I said, I plan to get her out here when the weather warms up." He hugged her closer. "I just realized something. Your bathrobe feels almost as soft as your mitten."

Clearly he was ready to move on from a difficult subject. She lifted her head. "Do you want to forget about the cider?"

"Oh, no, I think we should drink the cider. You have a table about five steps behind us. We can sit there and drink cider and talk dirty."

She laughed. "I don't know how."

"I don't believe that for a minute." Reaching around her, he picked up his mug. "I have my cider. Meet you at the table."

"It's a deal."

"See you there." He released her and seconds later, a chair scraped as he claimed one of her four kitchen chairs. "I'm set. Waiting for you, mitten lady."

So they were back to flirting and great sex. She took her mug of cider and turned around. By concentrating on the shifting shadows and light, she made out the spot Leo had claimed. She took the opposite chair.

His voice came out of the darkness. "Cowboys are supposed to help women into their seats, but if I tried, we might both go down."

"I've got this. I'm glad you didn't try."

"Is this cider leaded or unleaded?"

"Unleaded."

"Good. I want to keep my wits about me. What's left of them, anyway. Thanks for the cider, Fi. Ready to play this game?"

"I have no idea. You start."

"Okay. Here's to all things warm and juicy."

She lifted her mug and managed to connect with his. "To warm and juicy." She sipped her rapidly cooling cider.

"Your turn."

"Okay. Here's to all things firm and..." She couldn't come up with a second word.

"*Long-lasting.* That's the one you're looking for."

"I like *thick* better. Firm and thick."

He chuckled. "To firm and thick." He took a swallow and held out his mug. "To a long, hard ride." His voice grew husky toward the end.

Moisture dampened her lady parts. She tapped her mug against his. "To a long, hard ride."

He put down his cider and pushed back his chair. "Come with me, pretty lady. It's my turn with the mitten."

<u>19</u>

Leo stayed until almost twelve, but then he forced himself to leave Fiona's warm bed. They needed sleep and he could easily make love to her all night. He hadn't had this kind of stamina in years.

He dressed in the light from the Christmas tree while she lay in bed, tempting as hell. He moved fast, determined to get his clothes on before his willpower failed him.

"I still want to walk down with you."

He glanced over at her. "And I want to leave knowing you're snuggled under the covers, basking in the glow of your latest climax. That's why I asked for your spare key."

"And now you can let yourself in, too."

"I can."

"If you get finished with Garrett's Brotherhood initiation before I'm done with the celebration at Eva's, you could drive in and wait for me here."

"That has possibilities."

"You could be lying in bed, naked."

He laughed. "That's *not* a possibility."

"Why?"

"It's not manly."

"So what would be manly?"

"I don't know. Not that. But I'll be happy to drive in and wait for you here if I'm finished early. I'll switch on the tree and turn down the covers."

"Then what?"

"I'll think of something. But it won't be stripping down and jumping into bed. Count on it." Fastening his jeans, he zipped up and walked over to the bed. "Sleep well." Hand braced on the pillow, he leaned down and gave her a soft kiss.

At least it started out that way. She cupped the back of his head and tugged him closer. The kiss quickly spun out of control. Soon his tongue was in her mouth and his hand was cupping her breast.

The alarm on his phone snapped him out of a maneuver that would have involved taking off his pants again. Gasping, he extricated himself and staggered back. "I'm leaving. I really am."

She flopped back on the pillow, breathing fast. "What's that noise?"

"My alarm." He pulled his phone from his pocket and shut it off. "I set it for midnight in case… well, this."

"Smart."

Her breathless laughter made him smile. "I'm taking off. No more goodbye kisses. Want me to turn off the lights on the tree?"

"You can leave them on. They're almost like a nightlight. I love the tree. Thank you."

"You're welcome." He lingered a moment, gazing at her smile. Too bad she couldn't see his. Didn't want to, in fact.

He hurried through the door, calling out *goodnight* as he headed for the stairs.

* * *

Late the next afternoon, Leo grabbed a load of wood from the pile behind the bunkhouse and headed out to the fire pit. Nick followed with an armload of kindling and a couple of old issues of the *Gazette*.

Earlier they'd cleared the path and a spot in front of the pit with the Gator's snowplow attachment. Battery-operated lanterns were in place to light the way from the bunkhouse kitchen door. Rafe had brought the Adirondack chairs over from the cottage where Kate had been storing them for the winter.

In the kitchen, Jake and Garrett were making dinner with some help from CJ. Like old times, having everyone pitching in to create a Brotherhood event.

Nick crumpled up newspaper and arranged kindling on top. "Don't know if anybody's mentioned that the rest of us are planning to spend the night at the bunkhouse."

"You are? Even CJ?"

"Isabel begged us to take him off her hands for the night. His hovering is driving her nuts. Lucy, Millie and Kate are going to hang out with her."

"Poor CJ. I'd probably be in the same shape." An overnight was happening. That killed his plans with Fiona tonight, but if the Brotherhood was gathering, he'd be there. "So when did you guys decide this?"

"It was a spontaneous thing. Jake thought it seemed lame to initiate Garrett into the Brotherhood and then everybody takes off. He and Matt decided to stay. Rafe went along with the idea and I decided to do the same. CJ didn't want to, but we convinced him the women would have a good time together. We don't expect you to do it, though."

"But I will." He set several logs on top of the kindling and stacked the rest near the fire pit.

"Garrett doesn't want you to."

"Why?" He straightened and looked at Nick. "Is he mad at me?"

"No. He's rooting for you. He said you're making good progress with Fiona and you should go see her again tonight, keep the ball rolling."

"I appreciate that, but if the Brotherhood is doing an overnight, I—"

"You'll be here for the ceremony and you can stay for a drink around the fire pit afterward, but then we're kicking you out."

"What if I refuse to go?"

"We'll make you chug a root beer float."

He laughed. "I can't understand everybody's obsession with those things. The return trip to the dinosaur museum was terrific, but why you guys rave about those floats is beyond me."

"I'll bet Fiona loves 'em."

"Nah, she's smarter than that."

"Gonna go see her tonight?"

"It doesn't feel like the right choice, bro. We don't have these gatherings like we used to. I don't want to miss it."

"That's the other thing I meant to tell you. Matt suggested we schedule a monthly overnight. The Babes do it. Why shouldn't we?"

Leo smiled. "Just not on the same night."

"Actually, it should be. That way we're available if they get themselves into a snarl."

"Good point." He chuckled. "There have been snarls. Anyway, I like the idea of setting up a schedule, making it a regular thing."

"Feel better about going to see Fiona?"

"I guess. I was figuring on inviting her to Christmas dinner."

"Whoa, that's bold. I thought she wanted to keep your relationship in the dark, so to speak."

"She does, but she should be at the dinner. She was the Operation Santa elf. If we didn't have such a complicated relationship, Henri would have invited her by now. She told me as much today."

"I hadn't thought of that. Watching the video with everybody is a treat. Fiona shouldn't miss out, but after what you've said, I'm not sure she'll agree to it."

"Me, either, but I'll at least ask, let her think about it."

"I wish you luck." Nick glanced at the logs stacked next to the fire pit. "We'd better haul more wood out here. I have a feeling we'll keep that fire going for a while."

Leo followed him back to the wood pile and loaded up. "Hey, I wanted to ask you something about the initiation. Matt's using Henri's iPad to show the video of Charley, right?"

"That's what he said." Nick sorted through the pile and chose a few massive logs. "These should burn a while." Hoisting them into his arms, he headed back toward the path.

"Has he checked the temperature range of that thing?" Leo fell into step beside him.

"He did. Two nights ago the iPad wouldn't have worked out here, but we'll be at least ten degrees warmer tonight. It's a short video. Should be fine."

"Do you remember it?"

Nick exhaled. "Yeah."

"It'll be intense, seeing it again."

"That's another thing Matt suggested. It wouldn't be so intense if we'd watched it a few times since the funeral. But we haven't. Henri's seen it a bunch of times. Matt thinks we should watch it every year." He added his wood to the pile Leo had started.

Leo stacked his on top. "Maybe we should. Doesn't help us this time, though."

"But it's the right thing for the initiation. Garrett needs to see it."

"Yep." Maybe he did, too. He could use a dose of Charley's wisdom.

Nick surveyed the wood supply. "That should do it. Let's go get some chow. I'm starving."

"Wow, really? That's so unlike you."

The meal was a boisterous affair fueled with jokes and bottles of hard cider. Leo only drank one bottle with dinner, pacing himself. He needed to be alert tonight.

While the rest of the Brotherhood worked on cleanup, he volunteered to walk the path and turn on the lanterns. He couldn't say he was looking forward to the video. He'd almost said something to Garrett about the emotional impact so the guy wouldn't be blind-sided.

Except it likely wouldn't affect Garrett that much. He hadn't known Charley. Leo gazed up at the sky full of glittering stars and took a deep breath. "Hey, Charley, am I doing the right thing, asking Fiona to Christmas dinner? Henri says I am."

An owl hooted nearby.

"I'll take that as a yes." He headed back into the kitchen. Cleanup was over and everyone was tugging on jackets and hats.

Matt picked up Henri's tablet and started for the back door. "Let's do this. Garrett, you're with me."

Garrett hesitated. "You're not going to blindfold me?"

Matt turned back. "Why would I?"

"I thought that's what usually happened in this kind of deal."

"Then I guess it won't be your typical initiation ceremony. No blindfold. No secret handshake, no—"

"I've always thought we needed a secret handshake." CJ glanced around. "Anybody else want one?"

"Not me." Rafe settled his hat on his head. "One more damn thing to remember and sure as the world I'd forget what we decided and do it wrong."

"We don't need one, anyway," Nick said. "Secret handshakes are for when you're spread out over the state, or over the country, maybe even over the world. It's a way to recognize who's in the group and who isn't."

"Yeah, okay." CJ grabbed his hat and his phone. After glancing at it, he tucked it in his jacket pocket. "I still think it would be cool."

"We'll take it under advisement," Matt said, "for when we go global." He opened the kitchen door and walked down the cement steps to the cleared path.

Normally it would be a noisy procession, but tonight nobody spoke. When they reached the fire pit, Matt asked Garrett to light the bonfire. It caught right away, which Leo took as a good sign. An easel stood nearby. Matt set the tablet on it.

Leo glanced at him. "Lucy's contribution?"

"She made me promise we'd return it in the condition we got it." His breath created puffs of fog. "Garrett, this video speaks for itself, or rather, Charley speaks for himself." His voice got a little thicker with those last few words. He coughed and cleared his throat.

Leo stared at the ground. From the corner of his eye, he caught his brothers doing the same.

Then Matt soldiered on. "We lost him to a massive heart attack four years ago." He swallowed, but when he continued, his tone was stronger. "He was a mentor, friend and father to us, and we formed the Brotherhood as a tribute to him. That's why we decided our creed would be *What would Charley do?*"

Garrett nodded. "Easy to remember."

"Tough to follow," Jake said.

"Very tough," Matt said. "Charley set a high bar. But when we succeed in living up to his example, I think he knows." He tapped the screen and Charley's beloved face filled it.

Leo sucked in a quick breath as grief hit him hard. Charley's smile creased his tanned cheeks and crinkled his eyes until they were almost closed, but the sparkle peeked through. He looked so happy and vital, so damn real.

Hey, there! Don't see the point in doing this, but Henri seems to think I'm mortal like everybody else.

Charley's warm, gruff voice reached deep into Leo's chest, wrapped around his heart and squeezed. Could he take this? He glanced at his brothers. Lots of blinking going on.

Making a video about my philosophy sounds presumptuous to me, but that woman's persistent as hell. I love that about her.

Leo gulped.

So here goes. The Golden Rule still fits most any situation, in my book. Do unto others as you'd have them do unto you. Be truthful. Be kind. Be fair. Keep your word. Basic stuff. I didn't invent any of it.

And for God's sake, don't take yourself too seriously. Look for reasons to laugh, especially at yourself, and you'll find a million of 'em. Don't get so busy that you forget to look at the mountains or the sunrise. Life is beautiful. People are beautiful. Count your blessings and love one another.

He glanced off camera. *Henri? Is that enough?*

Henri's words were too faint to understand but clearly she'd reminded him of something.

Oh, yeah. Have a hell of a good time! Every damn day! I sure do!

The video ended.

The crackling of the fire blended with throat clearing and coughing. Leo scrubbed both hands over his face. They came away wet. Pulling his bandana from his back pocket, he wiped his eyes.

Matt took a shaky breath. "Garrett, think you want to join us in living up to Charley's legacy?"

"Yes, I do." Garrett's voice wasn't all that steady, either. "It'll be an honor. Charley must have been a fine man. I wish I'd known him."

"I wish you had, too." Matt offered his hand. "Welcome to the Buckskin Brotherhood."

20

"A touch more, Fi?" Eva held the bottle poised over her wine glass.

"Sure. Thanks to Jared, I don't have to drive home."

"Same here." Beth held out her glass for a refill. "Remember last year? Christmas Eve? Good thing we didn't have to drive anywhere that night."

"Oh, my God." Eva made a face. "Mistletoe martinis. Wicked good, but they put you under the table before you know what's happening."

"And while you were sipping mistletoe martinis, I was in Thailand with my folks. It's hard to believe there was a time I barely knew you guys."

"Isn't that the truth?" Eva gazed at her. "You hadn't opened the shop yet, right?"

"I decided to wait until after the New Year so I could have one more vacation with my parents. I'm glad I did, but now that I've experienced Christmas in Apple Grove, I can't imagine being anywhere else."

"I can't either." Beth settled back in her chair and sipped her wine. "Especially now that Eva has this fabulous house. You've inspired me with the amazing decorating job, girlfriend. The little Victorian village on the mantle, especially. And the vintage ornaments on your tree."

"I love it all," Fiona said. "The pine boughs, the wooden Santa and sleigh, the stockings, the teddy bears, the holiday throw. If I'd grown up with this version of Christmas, I'd be a fan."

"You can thank Winifred Barton. All I added were the fresh pine boughs and the tree, of course. Since I'd been here for Christmas tea several times, I tried to get it as close as I could to how she had the place decorated."

"Where did she store the rocking horse?" Fiona had been eyeing the sweet little wooden horse ever since she'd arrived. "That couldn't have fit in any of the boxes."

"It does when you take it apart. It's sturdy, too. A kid could ride that thing."

Beth laughed. "Then you and Nick need to get busy and make a kid."

"That's definitely on the table."

Fiona sent her a teasing glance. "I hope you moved the candlesticks first."

Eva blushed. "That isn't what I meant."

"But I'll lay you odds they've made whoopee on this table, Fi. Look at her face."

"Whoopee, yes, if you must know. But not babies. Not yet. I'm old-fashioned enough to want a wedding first."

Beth's eyebrows rose. "Is that an announcement of impending nuptials?"

"Nope. But Nick's got something up his sleeve. He keeps looking at me and smiling."

"He's always done that," Fiona said. "He's besotted."

"I mean he's smiling more than usual. Like he has a secret."

Beth nodded. "It's that time of year."

Fiona glanced at her. "Do you think Jared might—"

"Not at this stage. We still haven't figured out if we're going to live together. I love my little apartment and he loves the ranch. That makes it complicated."

"I understand." Eva's gaze took in the areas she'd lovingly decorated. "Luckily, Nick wanted to move here. If he'd suggested building a place on Buckskin land like some of his brothers have..."

"He wouldn't do that," Beth said. "He knows how you feel about this house. Jared's not pushing me to move out to the ranch, either. I'm looking forward to spending Christmas Day there, but I'll look forward to coming home again, too." She glanced over at Fiona. "That reminds me, are you still going to the graveyard on Christmas?"

"I am."

"You have to text me if you see anyone, especially if you recognize the person."

"Me, too," Eva said. "Can you text us both? I'll be at Henri's house with the Buckskin gang, but I'll check my phone."

"Which is the other thing I meant to ask you, Fi," Beth said. "If you're going to stake out the graveyard at dusk, what about Christmas dinner at the Buckskin?"

She blinked. "What about it?"

"Operation Santa. I was invited last year because I was the elf. Didn't I tell you about that part?"

"If you did, I spaced it."

"It's not the dinner so much as the video they show after the meal, the one from the kids' parents. It's so sweet."

"That's when they watch it? I knew about the video but no one's contacted me about dinner."

"Well, this year was different, since Leo took over from Ben, so maybe that's why you haven't heard anything."

"I'm guessing that's exactly why. I'll bet people are confused about whether to ask me or not." She looked at Eva. "Have you heard any talk about the video or dinner?"

"No, but I'm the new kid in the Buckskin gang. I don't always get the scoop. Want me to ask Nick?"

"No. I'll talk to Leo about it. I'd love to see the video, but—"

"You're afraid being with Leo in broad daylight will turn you into a blithering idiot." Eva looked sympathetic.

"Yep."

"I personally don't think that would happen," Beth said gently. "But if going would stress you out..."

"It would. You should have seen me when we had dinner at the Moose. It was pathetic."

"Probably not as bad as you think it was," Eva said, "but since then you've spent hours with the man. Can't you come at it from that perspective?"

"What a great idea. When we're with the Buckskin gang and I'm feeling tongue-tied and awkward, I'll just picture him naked. What could go wrong?"

Eva choked down her wine and grabbed a napkin to blot her mouth. "Yeah, don't picture him naked."

"They served liquor during Christmas dinner," Beth said. "You could—"

"There you go. I'll be the elf who got smashed on Christmas. Why didn't I think of that?"

"Talk to Leo," Eva said. "Maybe he'd wear the Santa suit if you asked him."

Fiona grinned. "Because *that* wouldn't be weird. I love both of you for trying to come up with solutions, but I think I'll just skip the dinner, assuming I'm invited. Way too much stress involved at this stage of our relationship. Maybe Leo can get me a link so I can see the video on my computer. I'll talk to him about it tonight."

* * *

Eva had made a Yule log for dessert. Fiona had never tasted one and instantly fell in love with the rolled chocolate cake, creamy mousse and dark chocolate frosting that mimicked the texture of bark. "I've been missing out on Yule logs all these years, too." She scraped the last of her portion from a vintage china plate with a holly and ivy design. "Christmas is rapidly becoming my favorite holiday."

"Especially in Apple Grove," Beth said. "This town does Christmas right."

"Sure seems like it." Fiona's phone pinged. She'd tucked it beside her hip so she'd catch a text from Leo. "Excuse me a minute." She glanced at the message. "He's at my apartment. I guess that means Nick will be home soon."

"Actually, he's spending the night at the bunkhouse."

"He is?" She stared at Eva. "Why?"

"Brotherhood gathering. He said they'd decided it was appropriate since they were inviting someone in for the first time ever."

"Then why is Leo at my apartment?"

"Because he likes being with you?"

"Well, sure he does. I like being with him, but that shouldn't outweigh his connection with his brothers."

"I guess you can talk to him about that issue, too."

"Don't worry. I will." His decision unnerved her. They'd only spent two nights together. What was he thinking?

Beth picked up her phone. "I'll text Jared and see if he's ready to pick us up."

"You know what? If he's not, I could walk. It's only four blocks." She needed to talk to Leo ASAP.

"He'd be mortified if you did that. He's a cowboy." She said it as if that explained everything.

Which it did. Fiona hadn't lived in Apple Grove as long as Beth, but she'd learned that cowboys were big on keeping their word.

Beth's phone chimed. "He'll be here in five minutes."

Fiona and Beth used those five minutes to help Eva clear the table and load the dishwasher with whatever she dared put in there. Didn't end up being much.

"You've got a lot of dishes to wash by hand," Fiona said. "I don't like leaving you with—"

"Don't worry about it. I adore taking care of Winifred's things. Sharing them with you guys has been a blast. We should do a girls' night Christmas celebration every year."

"Absolutely," Beth said. "You have the premier setup in this house."

Fiona smiled. "Look at us. Establishing Christmas traditions. I never thought I would."

"But you're in Apple Grove, now," Eva said. "Establishing traditions is what we do best."

21

Fiona was on her way. The wind hadn't kicked up tonight, so he'd left the shop door unlocked.

Amazing how sitting in the semi-dark sharpened his hearing. He'd identified the rumble of Jared's badass truck when he'd pulled up in front. The motor of that big engine continued to vibrate as Fiona came through the door. Once she'd flipped the lock with a popping sound, Jared had backed out and headed away from town, the growl of his truck gradually fading.

Fiona's chair that she kept near the bedroom door was now over by the little tree. He'd moved it to give him a place to sit and wait for her. Perching on the bed fully clothed wasn't any sexier than waiting naked under the covers.

He'd angled the chair so the light didn't hit his face and startle her. Anticipation gripped him as she came up the stairs. And yearning. He was tired of living in the shadows. He wanted to see and be seen.

She appeared in the doorway, her face and body faintly lit by the Christmas tree. "Hi."

He stood. "Hi." The lights on the tree reflected on her pale hair and the gleam of a gold necklace at her throat. She wore a red dress made from some soft material that draped her figure.

She walked into the room, but paused several feet away. "Eva told me that the other members of the Brotherhood are staying at the bunkhouse tonight. Why didn't you?"

"I was going to, but after talking with Nick, I changed my mind."

Even in the dim light, her surprise was obvious. "Why?"

"I was there for the ceremony and stayed for a drink after it was over. I'd made plans with you."

"You could have cancelled them. I would have been okay with that."

"You would?" Disappointing that she was so casual about it.

"It doesn't seem right that you're with me instead of with your brothers."

"Want me to leave?" His chest tightened.

"Not really. That doesn't feel so great either."

The bands around his chest loosened. "Glad to hear it."

She took a deep breath. "I wonder if we should... clarify a few things."

"Like what?"

"Where we see this going. Since it's only our third night together, I wasn't too worried about it. But choosing to be with me instead of the Brotherhood—"

"It's not as big a deal as it sounds like. This was a spur-of-the-moment plan. Jake realized that after the ceremony and a little celebrating around the fire pit, everyone except Garrett would take off."

"And if you hadn't made plans with me, you would have been there."

"Except I did make plans with you." He crossed the room and reached for her, not sure if she'd let him pull her close.

But she relaxed into his arms, making that electric contact that jumpstarted his pulse. "Garrett wanted me to keep this date." He gazed into her shadowed face. "I'm glad I did."

"I'm glad you did, too." She rested her palms on his chest and her voice softened. "But just so you know, I have no expectations."

His breath hitched. "Meaning what?"

"You and I are spur-of-the-moment, too. I was going to send you on your way the night of Operation Santa. Until you kissed me."

"And you liked it." Leaning down, he brushed his mouth across hers. "I could tell."

"You rocked my world." Her arms wound around his neck and she nestled closer. "I wanted you bad."

He slid his hands down her back to her firm tush and settled her against his needy package. "Past tense?"

Her breath caught. "Present tense."

"Then let's do something about that." He'd encountered the dress's zipper on the way down. He returned to a spot between her shoulder blades, located the tab and gently pulled as he nibbled on her full mouth.

"I want to." She cupped his head in both hands and leaned away from his kiss. "But first I'd like to know we're on the same wavelength."

"Okay." When the zipper glided past her bra, he paused to unfasten the hooks. Then he kept going. "Start broadcasting and I'll tune right in."

"Hey." Her fingers pressed into his scalp. "This is important."

"And I'm listening." The zipper ended at the small of her back. He couldn't resist slipping his hands inside her dress. Where her panties should have been, he encountered warm bare skin and two thin strips of elastic, one at her hips and the other dipping down to disappear between her cheeks. "You're wearing a thong."

"I am, but before we—"

"Is it new?" He lovingly caressed her sleek bottom.

"Fairly new. Leo, I—"

"Thongs turn me on. How did you know that?"

"I'm psychic. Could we please—"

"I have an idea."

"Does it have anything to do with the part of you currently wedged up against me?"

"Good guess. How about if we make love first and then discuss the wavelength situation? Your thong just short-circuited my brain."

Her sigh of resignation had a hint of amusement. "Okay." She released him from her iron grip and he was finally able to kiss her and put some heat into it. Her dress and bra came off with almost no effort and she kicked off her shoes.

He scooped her into his arms, leaving the thong in place and her gold necklace on as he carried her to the bed and laid her down. Stripping off his clothes, he tossed them on the chair.

His body cast a shadow over her and he moved aside, the better to enjoy the vision that was Fiona. He longed to flood the room with light, but he had to make do with the faint glow from the tree.

It was enough. The face of a jolly Santa decorated the white satin thong. Grinning, he climbed into bed, braced his hands on either side of her head and leaned down, his mouth inches away from hers. "You bought that thong today."

"What makes you say that?" She cupped the back of his neck and urged him closer.

"It would have been wasted in the dark."

"Like it?"

"I'm about to show you how much." Capturing her mouth, he reached under the pillow for the condom he'd tucked there. He paused to roll it on before beginning a leisurely journey from her lips all the way down to her toes. He saved the treasures beneath the thong for last.

By the time he slipped it off, she was on the brink of coming. A few swipes of his tongue pushed her over the edge. Moving over her, he plunged deep and stroked fast to intensify her climax. Must have worked because she sounded very happy with his efforts.

As her cries began to subside, he shifted the angle and took her up again. This time, he joined her, sinking into her heat with a groan.

Riding the wave of his release, he gasped her name. Then he said it again, more slowly as he drifted back to earth. The rush of emotion that followed caught him unprepared. His throat tightened.

Damn. He'd never had *this* reaction to coming. He swallowed hard and rested his forehead against her shoulder. Squeezing his eyes shut, he prayed she wouldn't figure out how close he was to losing it.

She stroked his head as she trembled in the aftermath of her climax. "I did buy that thong today." She drew a shaky breath. "I thought you'd get a kick out of it."

"Mm." He didn't trust himself to speak.

"First thong ever. Not very comfortable."

"Bet not." His voice sounded raspy, like a guy on the verge of... whatever he was on the verge of. Unmanly behavior, that's for sure.

"Leo?"

"Hm?"

"Are you okay?"

"Yep." Still sounded like a frog. "Be back." He eased away from her, climbed out of bed and made his escape to the bathroom. She'd added something to the décor in there. A nightlight in the shape of a Christmas ornament sent out a soft red glow.

It allowed him to accomplish the cleanup job without turning on the overhead. Just as well. He didn't want to look in the mirror and see red-rimmed eyes. He blamed Charley's video for the state he was in.

Charley's video and then making love to Fiona. He was falling for her and she... he didn't know where she stood. She'd bought that thong to please him, but that only meant she was having fun with this adventure.

Tonight's climax had brought him to the brink of an emotional meltdown. Time to face facts. He'd never been in this for fun and games. He wanted something more lasting, like what Charley had found with Henri.

Armed with that insight, he walked back into the bedroom and settled in beside her, his back to the light from the tree.

She reached for his hand and wove her fingers through his. "I didn't ask you how the initiation went. It's probably a secret ceremony, so I don't expect you to give me details, but did it work out the way you all hoped?"

"It did, at least I think so. It's a private ceremony, but there's nothing secret about it. We showed him a video Charley made not long before he died."

"Was he sick? Did he know he was going to—"

"Not at all. Henri had bought a new video camera and wanted to test it. She coaxed him into talking about his philosophy of life. He didn't want to do it, but she kept after him until he agreed."

"You all must be glad to have it, now."

"We are, but the Brotherhood hasn't watched it since the funeral four years ago."

She squeezed his hand. "Tough?"

"Yeah." He took a steadying breath. "What is this thing you wanted to discuss earlier? My brain's in slightly better shape to process whatever it is."

"Maybe this isn't the time. You've already had a taxing evening."

"Is this a taxing subject?"

"I guess it could be."

The tightness in his chest had returned. "Is it important?"

"I think so."

"Then lay it on me."

"Okay." She took a deep breath. "I worry that we're not looking at this relationship the same way."

"How could we? We're two different people."

"Point taken. But if our views are widely divergent, then we—"

"Let's hope not. I never want to diverge widely with you. That sounds terrible." Maybe he could joke his way through this.

She exhaled. "We shouldn't go into it now."

"Sorry. Yes, we should. You said it was important." The voice of doom was sounding in his head, but he blocked it. Might as well get whatever this was over with.

"Well, all right. What if I give you my view of the relationship and you can see if it matches up with yours?"

It wouldn't. "Go ahead."

"To me you're like Zorro."

"What?"

"You know, the mystery man who wears a mask, like the Lone Ranger. You're this shadowy figure who shows up, makes fabulous love to me and leaves. You're a fantasy."

That stunned him. It put him in a box he didn't want to live in. "No, I'm not."

"Then how do you see things?"

"I'm a man who met a fascinating woman. She has a problem with my looks, so I'm dealing with that as best I can because I'm crazy about her. If I'm lucky, she'll conquer her issue and we'll have a shot."

"At what?"

"A real relationship, Fi. You have your fantasy and I have mine. I never aspired to be Zorro."

22

"I don't mean you're literally Zorro." Fiona scrambled to process Leo's last few comments. He wanted a shot at a real relationship. But what if she couldn't pull that off? Where did that leave them?

"That touched a nerve, I guess." He brought their joined hands to his mouth and kissed the tips of her fingers. "I spent way too much time in the acting world being someone else. I'm Leo Marston, working cowboy. That's who I am, not—"

"I promise I don't imagine Zorro is making love to me. I know it's you."

"Good."

"But I'm worried about the other thing you said. That part about a real relationship. I'm not sure I can—"

"Why not? Don't get me wrong. Making love in the dark is great. Making love in the light from the tree is even better. But I want more."

Her stomach bottomed out. "You could be disappointed."

"Not a chance." He stroked her palm with his thumb.

"You're fascinated by the person I am when we make love in the dark. I'm no longer intimidated by your handsome self. I turn into a *femme fatale*."

"I was fascinated with you when you were dressed as an elf. That wasn't in the dark."

"But you were in disguise. In a way, you still are."

"Are we back to Zorro?"

"No, forget about him. This is about me. In the shadows, I can be myself, especially making love. Shine a light on it and we could destroy what we have, what brought us together. I'm not sure I can be myself when we're in the light."

"Keep us in the dark and we have no future."

"I know." And she hated it.

He went silent for a beat. Then he dragged in a breath. "I want a future with you, Fi. That's why I put on the Santa suit."

"That still blows me away. You went to so much trouble just to—"

"It got me this far."

"What if this is as far as it goes?"

"I don't believe that. Which is why I want you to come to Christmas dinner at the Buckskin."

Thank goodness she'd discussed this with Beth and Eva so she'd had some time to frame a response. "So I can see the video?"

"Mostly. How did you—"

"Beth told me. She had a great time watching it last year."

"Last year's was good. I predict this one will be even better. I can't wait, especially because this time I know what's coming."

"I'd love to see it, but I don't need to be at Christmas dinner. Someone can forward the link to me. My email address is on my Planet-Friendly Paper website."

"I can get it for you, but that won't be half as good as watching it with everyone else...."

"I'd rather not, Leo."

"It'll be so rambunctious you'll be swept along by it. You'll forget all about—"

"I'm not chancing it."

"The Brotherhood wrapped all those packages and you should hear them whoop and holler when a kid opens one they wrapped and goes ballistic over the toy."

"I'm sure it's fun."

"Beyond fun. And you've met those kids and parents face-to-face. Do you want to miss watching Georgie open his presents? Or that firecracker of a little redheaded girl, Jackie? Or her little sister Molly? What about those two boys, Jay and Davey?"

"I won't miss it if someone sends me the link." The silence stretched between them.

"I want you to be there," he said at last. "Please think about it. You can come at the last minute. You don't have to notify anyone. You can just show up."

"Please don't expect me."

"All right, I won't expect you. If you don't make it, I'll get the link and send it to you."

"Thank you." She hesitated. "You're upset."

"Disappointed."

"Because you're hoping we can have a real relationship, as you called it?"

"Yes, ma'am."

"What if that never happens? Would you rather just—"

"No."

"But—"

"I don't want to break it off, Fi. I don't think I realized how much dinner at the Moose messed with your head. How embarrassed you were by... I almost want to call it stage fright."

She wouldn't know. She'd never been on a stage. "I don't want to be that frightened woman."

He gathered her close. "And I don't want to give you up. We can stay in the dark if that's what you need."

"But that's not fair to you. I can tell you're getting frustrated with it."

"I'll tell you what would frustrate me more." He cupped her breast and began a lazy massage. "Knowing you were climbing into bed alone every night and I wasn't allowed to be here."

His touch sent heat to every part of her body, setting fire to logic.

Moving his caress lower, he smoothed a palm over her stomach and reached between her thighs. "Would it frustrate you, lying alone in this bed, longing to hear my footsteps on the stairs?"

She sucked in a breath as he aroused her with knowing fingers. "Yes."

"Then let's not worry about what the future will bring and concentrate on making each other happy." Thrusting his fingers deep, he proceeded to make her very happy indeed.

* * *

She woke from a dream of walking out on a stage stark naked. No mystery where that dream had come from. She turned her head.

Leo stood by the bed fastening the metal button on his jeans. He pulled up the zipper slowly, as if trying to make as little noise as possible.

"You don't have to be quiet. I'm awake."

"Sorry. Next time I'll get dressed in the bathroom."

"I don't want you to sneak out of here without waking me. I like being able to tell you goodbye."

He chuckled. "Just saying it might work. Kissing you goodbye leads to trouble." He picked up his jacket from the chair. "The gang is going to the Moose for Christmas Eve. We're starting early, might be there by four-thirty or five."

"Good to know."

"Okay if I show up here around ten?"

"I was hoping you would."

"Don't suppose I can talk you into dropping by the Moose before that."

"No, I'm afraid you can't."

"Both your buddies will be there. We invited Jared and Beth to hang out with us."

"They should fit right in."

"So would—"

"Leo." She smiled. "Give it up."

"All right." He leaned down. "I want to kiss you, after all. Don't grab my head. Keep your hands to yourself."

She laughed. "Okay." She lifted her face to his.

He touched down gently, his lips soft against hers. Then he cupped her face in both hands and put a little more into the kiss. It stayed sweet for about two seconds. Then his tongue got involved.

By the time he groaned and dropped to his knees by the bed, she'd abandoned his rules and shoved her fingers into his thick hair. He pressed her back onto the pillow and thrust his tongue deep.

The trill of his phone alarm penetrated the sound of their ragged breathing. With an even louder groan, he ended the kiss and pushed himself to his feet. "Epic fail."

"Not my fault."

"It's mine. Zero willpower." Chest heaving, he backed away from the bed. "I don't know what it is about you."

"I do."

"I do, too. You're irresistible." His voice softened. "See you around ten, Fi. Maybe sooner."

"Looking forward to it."

He headed for the door. "If you change your mind about the Moose, just show up."

"I won't."

"Okay, then. See you soon." His steps beat a staccato rhythm as he bounded down the stairs. Her eager lover didn't see the obvious reason for his infatuation. Or didn't want to.

What if he found her irresistible because they only met during these late-night trysts? In the dark.

_**23**_

Lights glowed from the windows of the bunkhouse when Leo pulled in. He crossed to the front door, his boots crunching on the hard-packed snow in the parking area where several trucks sat, their windshields covered with ice. The scent of coffee and the sound of laughter drifted toward him on a frigid breeze.

Last winter this had been the normal routine as the Brotherhood started a new day. A wave of nostalgia washed over him. Good thing Matt had come up with the plan for monthly overnights.

He walked into a typical bunkhouse morning scene—the early birds slugging down coffee in the kitchen and telling jokes, the night owls, namely Jake and CJ, slowly dragging on their clothes. The wood stove was crackling and putting out heat. Leo quickly closed the door and took off his jacket.

Jake sat on his bunk wearing his jeans and a shirt which he hadn't buttoned yet. His bleary-eyed glance and lopsided smile were evidence of a late night and several bottles of cider. "Welcome home, bro."

CJ had ear buds in and his back to the door as he tucked in his shirt. He turned, plucked out the ear buds, shoved them in his pocket and grinned. "Greetings." Then he raised his voice. "Hey, bros. Lover boy just showed up."

The ruckus in the kitchen stopped as the coffee drinkers wandered out, mugs in hand. Nick's eyebrows lifted. "How'd it go?"

"Pretty damn obvious how it went," Rafe said. "His shirt's buttoned up wrong."

Leo checked. Yep. "Not a priority." He turned back to CJ. "Any word from Isabel?"

"She texted me about ten minutes ago. The women are having fun and she thinks Jake and I should stay and cook breakfast for you guys, give Garrett a break."

"That's fine," Garrett said, "but I don't want to sit and do nothing. I'll go down to the barn with the rest of you."

"Glad to have the help." Matt glanced around. "It'll be a gorgeous day. We could saddle up after we're done with breakfast and chores. Take a nice long ride."

Rafe nodded. "I'm in. And Kate will probably want to—"

"Right," CJ said. "The ladies will want to go, too, so I'll stay behind with Isabel."

"Not necessary, baby-daddy." Matt gave him a smile. "I just talked to Lucy and the ladies plan to hang out in their pajamas, paint their nails and watch Christmas movies until we all leave for the Moose."

"Count me out of the ride," Nick said. "Eva's finished at the salon at eleven, so after I help muck out stalls, I need to head on home."

"Oh, Nick, I forgot. That's the other part of Lucy's message. Eva's driving out here and bringing her nail polish. She has a better selection than the rest of them and she wants to watch movies, too."

Jake stood and joined the group. "I can take a hint. Vacation time has created a little too much togetherness. They want a break from our manly testosterone."

"Well..." Matt chuckled. "That's basically what Lucy said, but I was trying to be diplomatic."

"Yeah," CJ said, "but if we ride off into the wilderness, and Izzy goes into labor, what—"

"I'll put you in charge of monitoring cell service on the way out and back." Matt gazed at him. "We won't venture out far enough to lose it. We'll be notified if Isabel thinks it's time. And she'll have four capable women who can get her to the hospital if need be."

Rafe heaved a sigh. "Much as it pains me to admit this, they'd be calmer and more efficient than any of us."

"Good point." CJ rubbed the back of his neck. "Okay. I'll go. That's settled. I could use a cup of coffee if there's any left."

"I started a new pot." Garrett stepped aside to let him by. "Leo, you're probably ready for coffee."

"You know it." He followed CJ into the kitchen with Jake right behind him. "So what'd you guys do after I left?"

"The usual," Jake said. "Strippers, drugs, naked dancing by the fire. Like we do."

Matt came into the kitchen for a refill. "We played cards."

"Some of us better than others," Rafe called from the other room.

"So who was the big winner?"

"Garrett." Nick came through the door and walked over to the coffee pot. "He's a master of the bluff."

Garrett leaned in the doorway. "I got lucky."

"Oh, I think there's some serious skill involved." Matt lifted his coffee mug in Garrett's direction. "Well done."

"But enough about us." Nick poured himself some coffee. "Did you talk Fiona into coming to Henri's for Christmas dinner?"

"No." Leo nudged back his hat. "That first date was more traumatic than I realized. She's convinced hanging out with me under normal circumstances will make her freeze up like she did that night."

"But she was fine at Ed's party after the auction," Matt said.

"Because she drank a lot of Ed's champagne. I won't ask her to deliberately get wasted so she can navigate Christmas dinner."

CJ gazed at him. "What if you invite her to go to the Moose with us tonight? That would be kind of like Ed's party. She can have a few drinks, relax with all of us, maybe get over this."

"I mentioned it. She wasn't on board with the idea."

"There has to be a solution." Garrett sipped his coffee. "There always is."

"Hey." CJ stared at him. "That's freaky."

Matt nodded. "Very."

Garrett frowned in confusion. "What's freaky?"

Leo met his gaze. "Charley used to say that all the time."

"Yeah," CJ said. "And then sure as the world he'd come up with an answer."

"Goes to show you're one of us, bro." Leo gave him a smile. "You're quoting Charley without even knowing it."

* * *

Matt talked them into riding down to the barn in his truck.

"We're turning into pansies," Rafe complained from the front seat. "It's not *that* cold."

"Speak for yourself." Nick was wedged in the middle between Garrett and Leo. "Normally I'd object to being stuffed into the backseat like sardines, but it's nice and toasty back here."

Rafe snorted. "I'm surprised you didn't bring your blankie and your teddy bear."

"Speaking of teddy bears." Matt glanced in the rearview mirror. "I've heard all about how the disguise worked out, but what about Operation Santa? What can we look forward to on the video tomorrow?"

"You'll love it. This one family came out on the front porch and sang *We Wish You a Merry Christmas.* And there was this little redheaded girl,

Jackie, who is going to be president of something one of these days. Could be a big company. Maybe even president of the country."

"Just had an idea," Garrett said. "Did you take the Santa suit to the cleaners yet?"

"Haven't gotten around to it, why?"

"I might have a plan that would work, but you'll need the suit."

"I see where he's going with this," Nick said. "You could wear it for Christmas dinner. Fiona might come if you—"

"I doubt that would help as much now that she knows it's me. Besides, I couldn't eat with it on. I'd make a mess of the beard and I might spill on the suit. Thanks for the thought, though."

"You're right about the drawbacks," Garrett said. "I'll keep thinking."

"I appreciate it, but I doubt this will be a quick fix, no matter what I do."

"You never know." Nick pulled on his gloves as Matt brought the truck to a slow stop in front of the barn. "It's Christmas, after all."

<u>24</u>

Fiona wandered over to the front window of her apartment for the millionth time and gazed across the square. Christmas lights strung around the entrance and the street-side windows of the Choosy Moose reflected on the row of trucks parked diagonally in front of the bar.

Leo's wasn't one of them. Either he wasn't there—doubtful—or he'd parked in the back lot. Why not in front of her place? That would have made more sense.

She checked her phone. Almost nine. Would he decide to head over earlier than ten? With her windows closed tight, she couldn't hear the music from here, but by now the place would be rocking.

Every so often the door opened and she held her breath. Then a couple would come out and hurry down the sidewalk toward one of the trucks parked there.

Leo was still inside, joking with his brothers, maybe sipping a bottle of hard cider. Or he might be dancing. Line dancing at the very least. That had been a popular choice at the party following the auction.

Nick's truck sat close to the entrance and Jared's was a couple spaces down. Would Eva and Beth order mistletoe martinis tonight? Guaranteed those two would be dancing. They'd—

Wait. Was that Leo? Her heartbeat sped up. Sure did look like him, but instead of walking in her direction, he took off down the sidewalk and veered right at the alley leading to the back parking lot.

He must have bought her a gift and had gone to get it before he came over. She'd debated whether to give him one and had settled on a bottle of flavored body oil. She'd tucked it into a small gift bag and had left it under the little tree.

She stayed by the window watching for him to come back. Instead her phone pinged with a text.

Would you be willing to take a Christmas Eve stroll around the square with Santa?

She gulped. Change of plans. Alarm bells jangled. He was up to something, but what? She took a guess. *Followed by a brief stop at the Moose?*

That's one option. We could pop in for a minute so you could see the decorations. Or we can go back to your place.

Popping in could go south fast.

Just a stroll, then. It's nice out tonight, not too cold. I'll have the suit and the beard.

So he'd gone to his truck for the suit. *But I'll know it's you.*

And you know it's me in the dark. What do you say, Galadriel?

He would have to call her that. It was a reminder of the fun they'd had, but he'd likely meant it as a challenge, too. Galadriel was very brave.

She wanted to be. In the end, that tipped the scales. She could handle a walk around the square if that would make him happy. But going into the Moose would probably be too much.

She took a deep breath and typed a response. *I can be ready in five minutes.*

Great. Meet you by the gazebo.

See you there.

Dashing back to her bedroom, she flipped on the overhead, threw off her bathrobe and grabbed underwear out of her dresser drawer. She chose a sweater, jeans and boots.

Although he'd said it wasn't that cold, she put on her red wool coat, a plaid scarf, her red knit hat and gloves. She was from Phoenix, after all. When she walked out the front door, music from the Moose provided a distant soundtrack. A quick glance toward the gazebo revealed a slimmed-down version of Santa leaning against the railing.

Turning, she fumbled the door-locking process, her rapid breathing fogging the air. *Get a grip, girl.* At last the lock clicked and she put the key in her coat pocket.

Leo's gaze held hers as she cut across the square. He'd left off the glasses. The Christmas tree in the gazebo combined with the streetlamps provided a surprising amount of light. The closer she came, the more mesmerizing those blue eyes were.

She paused a few feet away to catch her breath. "You've lost weight, Santa."

"Cut out carbs."

"Switched to Western boots, too, I see."

"Always wanted to be a cowboy." He stepped toward her and held out his gloved hand. "Thanks for agreeing to take a walk with me."

"You're welcome." She put her hand in his and absorbed the familiar jolt of energy that surged whenever they touched. "If you hadn't worn those fake glasses during Operation Santa, I would have recognized you."

"Think so?" Squeezing her hand, he headed back across the square to the street.

"I know so. That electric blue makes an impression."

"I have the specs in my pocket. Want me to put them on?"

She hesitated. Her heart was racing, but maybe she'd get it under control in a minute. "Not yet. I'll let you know."

"Okay. Might as well walk in the street. Nobody's driving around tonight." Stepping onto a pavement shiny with melted snow, he led her away from her shop.

Away from safety. Her stomach churned. "I think the whole town's at the Moose."

"That's about right. Wall-to-wall people. The dance floor's packed, too."

"Did you dance?"

"A couple of line dances. It's a Brotherhood tradition, especially on Christmas Eve. Gotta do *Run, Rudolph, Run.*"

"Is the Buckskin gang still there?" The music was fainter, now.

"So far nobody's bailed. CJ made noises about taking Isabel home early, but she doesn't want to go. Ben keeps hinting that something special's coming up soon, so she wants to stay until whatever it is happens."

"Should you be out here with me? You could miss it."

"He said it wouldn't be for another twenty minutes or so."

Her pulse rate spiked. "Leo, I don't think I'm ready to go in there with you."

"What if I put on the glasses?"

"I'm not sure that would—"

"I'll put 'em on and you can see what you think." He let go of her hand and paused to dig them out of his pocket. He carefully slid them on without disturbing his beard. Then he turned. "Better?"

Light reflected off the lenses, obscuring his eyes. Her anxiety level dipped a little. "I guess so."

He took her hand. "Let's keep walking while you think about it. I'd hate for you to miss Christmas Eve at the Moose, and whatever this thing is Ben's talking about."

"You know it's not just going in there, right? It's going in with you and remembering what that felt like last time." Down the block, someone came out of the Moose and the beat of a country tune poured from the open door until it closed again, muffling the sound. She shivered.

"But I'm wearing the suit."

"You're not Clark Smith anymore, though."

"I thought maybe going into the Moose tonight would be a good transition. Then you'd feel better about going to Henri's tomorrow, at least to watch the video with all of us."

"You know what? I'm not sure I could go to Henri's anyway." An obvious reason had been staring her in the face. "I have something I need to do and I don't know how long it'll take."

"What?"

She hesitated. "If I tell you, you have to promise to keep it to yourself. Well, I guess Nick and Jared already know, but it can't go any farther."

"I won't say anything."

"Okay, then." She gave him a brief overview of her quest to identify Miss Barton's secret lover.

"Wow, that's quite a story. Nick's definitely keeping mum. He hasn't said a word about this."

"I'm glad to hear it. Even if I find out who it is tomorrow evening, I'll only tell Eva and Beth. I'm sure Nick and Jared will hear it from them and I'll tell you, too, but it can't become town gossip. That would be so unfair."

"How long will you stay out there waiting?"

"I'm not sure." She glanced ahead and her stomach tightened. The Moose was only a few yards away.

"It'll be cold sitting in your car."

"I'll run the heater every so often. And maybe take a hot drink in a thermos." This close, the lyrics of the song came through loud and clear. The band was playing *Grandma Got Run Over by a Reindeer* and the crowd was clearly into it.

"I hope you find out after all the digging you've done."

"Thanks. I hope so, too. I—"

"Leo!" Nick came out the door, coatless, and hurried toward them. "Hey, Fiona, good to see you." He turned to Leo. "Listen, bro, I was hoping I wouldn't have to search the square."

"What's up?"

"You'll want to get in here. Ben finally told us the surprise and it's about to happen."

"What is?"

"Henri and Ben are going to sing a duet."

25

Leo stared at Nick. "You're kidding!"

"Nope. Ben just told me so I ran out to see if you were nearby. Thank God you were right here."

Fiona's grip tightened. "Is this another tradition?"

"It sure isn't," Nick said. "This is a first. You—"

"I'll walk you home, Fi." He had no choice. Her deer-in-the-headlights expression didn't bode well.

"That's okay." She let go of his hand. "You don't have to. I can—"

"Nick?" Eva burst through the door, also without a coat. The sparkles in her hair and on her cheeks caught the lamplight. "Oh, good, you found them! Fi, come on. This is epic."

"I'm not sure I—"

"You'll hate yourself if you miss this, girlfriend. You really will."

Eva's enthusiasm seemed to work where his logic had failed.

"Okay, let's go." Without looking at him, she joined Eva, who immediately started chattering away as she ushered Fiona inside.

Nick sighed. "She didn't look totally okay with this."

"She's not, but maybe if she has Eva..."

"Let's think positive, Santa." He smiled. "Glad I got a preview of you in the suit. Garrett said you were something to behold."

"Yeah. Come on. I need to check on Fiona." He started for the door.

Nick followed him in. "My recommendation? Don't hover. Let Eva handle it."

"Good advice." He wound his way through the tables to the area commandeered by the gang. They'd saved his seat next to Millie and had managed to cram in one on his other side for Fiona. She'd taken off her coat and draped it over the back of the chair.

Eva sat next to her, clearly giving her a pep talk. She kept her voice so low he couldn't make out what she was saying. Not that she'd want him listening in.

Besides, he had his hands full with his brothers. They felt obliged to carry on, at max volume, about how fabulous he looked in the suit. And he began to sweat. Concern about Fi was part of it, but the polyester suit over his shirt and jeans worked outside. Inside, not so much, especially with a packed house.

When the Brotherhood finally abandoned the subject of his outfit, Jake leaned around Millie. "Hey, bro. Do you reckon Henri and the Babes will sound better than they do on karaoke night?"

"Hope so. I think Henri might pull it off, but if the Babes are singing backup, I have my doubts about the outcome."

"Me, too. I'll clap and shout and holler regardless, but—"

"You *all* will," Millie said. "I don't care if they sound like tomcats on a back fence. You're all gonna react like it's Faith Hill and Tim McGraw up there, with backup from Dolly, Reba, Martina, Trisha and the Judds."

Jake nodded. "Yes, ma'am. We know that."

"Lucy didn't say a word to me." Matt sat on Millie's far side. Clearly dumbstruck, he gazed at his wife as she joined the other Babes on the bandstand. "She has a pretty good voice, but I'm going with what Jake said about the karaoke nights."

"Yeah." Jake chuckled. "Remember the night the coyotes started howling along with them? It was a tossup as to who sounded—"

"Shh." Millie put a hand on Jake's arm. "They're getting ready to start."

Sweat trickled down the side of Leo's face. He unbuckled the wide black belt and opened his coat. Better. Except when he glanced at Fi, she was watching him. She looked nervous.

He leaned toward her and kept his voice down. "I'm just a little—"

"I can see you're sweating." She swallowed. "You should take off the coat."

He wasn't going to chance it. "I'm okay." He left the coat on and focused on Henri and Ben.

They each held a cordless mic as they walked to the front of the bandstand. If they were rattled, it didn't show.

The lights gleamed on Henri's short gray hair and Ben's snowy mop that he kept long enough to touch his collar. They wore matching Western shirts in Christmas green.

Their fond expressions as they glanced at each other brought a lump to his throat. If Henri couldn't have Charley, he was glad she'd let herself fall in love with Ben.

Ben addressed the crowd. "We've all been together a lot of years, and during that time I've hesitated to foist my singing on the good people of Apple Grove. But I like to sing, and so I decided—to paraphrase Lesley Gore—it's my bar and I'll sing if I want to."

Leo chuckled and snuck a glance at Fi. She'd smiled at that. Good sign.

"And I want to sing," Ben continued. "especially because Henri consented to a duet. For the past couple of Christmas seasons, I've thought of her whenever I've heard this tune. Couldn't tell her. But this year I can. The Babes graciously agreed to provide backup. Hope you like it. Here's our version of *All I Want for Christmas Is You.*"

Leo and his brothers whistled and stomped louder than anyone in the room. Millie gave them an approving glance.

The band played the intro and Henri began to sing. Leo's breath caught. The woman could *sing.* Then Ben joined in and the Babes swayed and crooned perfectly in tune.

Leo reached for Fiona's hand under the table and wove his fingers through hers. He loved this song and couldn't help moving in time to it. Fi moved a little, too. Having everyone's attention focused on the stage seemed to have settled her down. Soon the entire Buckskin contingent was in motion.

Toward the end, Leo stood and coaxed Fiona up, too. The wave traveled across the Brotherhood and continued through the rest of the audience until everyone was standing and swaying to the beat. Ben and Henri faced each other, singing their hearts out, oblivious to anything else.

Leo swallowed as joy spread through the crowd. Beautiful.

The song ended and Ben pulled Henri into a tight hug as the crowd roared its approval. They turned, arms around each other's waist, and blinked as if startled by the standing ovation. Then they laughed and bowed in unison.

Shouts of *more, more, more* earned a shake of the head from Ben. When the noise abated, he lifted the mic. "We practiced for hours on that. We don't have a repertoire, at least not yet. But stay tuned. This was fun. We just might do it again."

Amid more enthusiastic applause, he and Henri turned and exchanged high-fives with the Babes before all of them exited the bandstand.

The band launched into another song, but no one was on the floor. Everyone in the place had converged on Henri and Ben. Leo headed toward them, too, running interference so Fiona wouldn't be caught in the crush.

Eventually he made it through the crowd, tugging her along behind him. He kept her hand tightly in his as he reached the stars of the evening. "You two blew me away. The Babes did, too."

Henri gave him a quick hug. "Thanks, Santa. I see you brought this year's Christmas elf along." She gave Fiona a smile.

Fiona returned it. "You were wonderful. Great."

"We worked hard on it," Ben said. "Ed brought over a voice coach from LA, which helped a ton."

"I was terrified, anyway." Henri glanced at Ben. "This guy wouldn't let me back out."

He grinned. "Are you sorry?"

"I *loved* it. At least after the first ten seconds when I was shaking like a leaf."

Fiona stared at her. "You were scared?"

"I was, but then we started, and I could tell Ben was having a blast. Something just gave way inside me. I didn't want to waste such a special moment being scared."

"I can't believe we didn't know," Leo said.

"I can't believe you didn't figure it out, since I was gone so much with no explanation."

"We just thought you were sneaking off to be with Ben."

"I was. We practiced mostly at Ed's, since the voice coach was staying with her." She looked over at Fiona. "I love my journal, by the way. If I fill this one, and I might at the rate I'm going, I'll need another one."

"I have more."

"Great." She hesitated. "Leo mentioned you might not make it tomorrow. I'm sorry to hear that, but if you change your mind, please come. No need to notify me. It's a buffet. Very casual. We'll start around five."

"I appreciate the invitation."

Leo slipped his arm around her waist. She was trembling. "We should move aside. People are lining up behind us."

"Right."

That one tense syllable told him so much. Fi was in trouble.

Henri beamed at them. "You need to dance to this one. They're playing an appropriate tune."

"So they are." He hadn't paid attention to the song the band was playing until now. It was Keith Urban's *I'll Be Your Santa Tonight.*

Leo gave Fiona's waist a squeeze as they maneuvered back toward the table. "We don't have to dance. We can leave."

"No, let's dance." Her tone was clipped.

"Why?"

"Because I don't want to look like some scared rabbit running away to hide." The words came out in a rush as she stared at the floor. "Now that I'm here, we should dance at least once. And you should take off your coat. And your glasses."

"But—"

"Please, Leo. The longer you leave stuff on, the more ridiculous I feel."

"Should I take off the beard, too?"

"Maybe not."

"Okay." He took off the glasses and put them in the coat pocket. Slipping out of it, he left it at the table and led her to the dance floor. "We can go back to your place after this."

"That's fine."

He drew her into his arms and she rested her cheek against his, likely to avoid gazing into his eyes. He sighed and pulled her closer. The tension began to ease from her body as she tucked in.

Relax, Fi. I've got you.

<u>26</u>

The slow, sexy tune settled over Fiona, gradually replacing her anxiety with the sensual pleasure of Leo's warm body pressed against hers. He gathered her close and moved to the beat, her hand held against his chest, their hips aligned.

He moved his head a fraction and his beard tickled her cheek. She giggled, nervous tension making the sound higher pitched than normal.

"Does it tickle?"

"A little. It's okay." She snuggled closer, blocking out her surroundings. "More than okay."

"Not as soft as the mitten, though."

"Nope." She closed her eyes and concentrated on his breathing blending with hers, the solid feel of his chest, the shelter of his broad shoulders and strong arms. The lights, the laughter, the murmur of voices and the clink of glasses faded. There was only the music and Leo.

Sexual hunger teased her, gliding through her body. She absorbed the thump of his heartbeat. His breath feathered the side of her neck and her hips brushed his. Desire simmered just under the surface.

They'd started dancing halfway through the song, so it ended before she was ready for the moment to be over. She stood still, eyes closed, holding onto the magic just a little bit long—

"Clear the way!"

A booming voice jerked her out of her romantic fog.

Leo released her and turned. "Oh, God." Grabbing her hand, he headed toward CJ, who had a grim-faced Isabel in his arms.

Isabel was putting up a fight as Rafe and Matt forged a path through the crowd. "Stop this nonsense, all of you. I can walk, damn it!"

"Not on my watch!" CJ kept going.

Henri pushed her way up to Isabel and tucked a jacket around her. Garrett came along behind CJ and draped a shearling coat over his shoulders.

Gripping Fiona's hand, Leo made his way through the confusion to Garrett. "She's in labor?"

"Her water broke. Rafe and Matt are taking them to the hospital. Everybody's headed there. Matt asked me to gather up Lucy, Kate and any of the Babes who need a ride. See you there." He worked his way back toward the group of tables.

See you there? Fiona's breath caught as icicles of fear stabbed her chest.

"Hey, bro." Nick hurried up with Eva. "You and Fiona can come with us. I'm parked right in front. We just have to fetch our coats."

Leo glanced quickly at her. "Is that—"

"It's fine." What else could she say? He'd never let her walk home alone so he could race to the hospital with the Buckskin gang. Besides, Isabel was a friend, someone she admired for her grit. She couldn't turn tail and run.

He flashed her a look of gratitude. "Thanks. I'll get our coats. Meet you guys by the front door."

Eva looped an arm over her shoulders as they hurried toward the entrance. "Hang in there. It'll work out."

"Yep."

"Why don't you wait by the door for Leo? Nick and I will go warm up the truck."

"Okay." Her stomach churned as she stood beside the door while others from the Buckskin gang hurried past. Several paused to ask if she needed a ride. She smiled and shook her head. The bulk of the crowd had remained and the band launched into *Rockin' Around the Christmas Tree.*

Leo showed up, her coat over his shoulder as he belted the Santa jacket. "Where'd they go?"

"They're warming up the truck." His beard was askew and his blue eyes were more intense than ever. The disguise wasn't working anymore, but now wasn't the time to tell him.

He helped her into her coat. "Are you okay?"

"Yes. Come on." If she kept moving, she'd get through it.

He ushered her out the door. "This might not take long."

"We'll see." She prayed it wouldn't, mostly for Isabel's sake, but also for hers.

An arm around her shoulders, Leo hustled her over to Nick's vintage truck, which was a two-door with a cramped back seat. Nick jumped out and flipped down his seat so Fiona could climb in.

Leo followed her. "Thanks for the ride, bro."

"Seemed obvious." He pulled the seat into place, got behind the wheel and closed the door. "We're the only ones who live in town, so we can bring you two back here when this is over."

"How long do you think it'll take?" He reached for her hand and enclosed it in both of his.

Nick backed the truck out of the parking space. "Not my area of expertise, but Eva was with the ladies for most of the day, so she might have info."

"It's impossible to predict." Eva turned in her seat. "We went online today, thinking we'd find some averages for first babies. No such thing. Some take forever to be born, and others pop right out."

"Cleo Marie will pop right out," Leo said. "At least she will if she's anything like her mother."

Fiona smiled, but it felt more like a grimace. "That's for sure." The dark interior of the truck gave her a temporary respite. The hospital would be bright, though.

"I know, right?" Eva said. "I was amazed that she was working at Cup of Cheer when you and I met Beth for coffee two days ago."

"I think it's way cool that this is happening on Christmas Eve." Nick picked up speed as he headed out of town. "I've heard kids born during the holidays have their birthdays swallowed by everything else going on, but that won't happen with Cleo Marie." He glanced in the rearview mirror. "Right, bro?"

"I can't imagine it. CJ and Isabel won't let that happen and Henri definitely won't."

"Henri's amazing," Eva looked over at Nick. "Wasn't that duet incredible?"

"Sure was. Wondered if they'd ever get together, let alone sing a duet at the Moose on Christmas Eve."

"My money has been on Ben all along," Eva said. "He's been patiently waiting for Henri to come around."

Nick turned onto the road leading to Apple Grove General. "If you ask me, patience is highly overrated. It's been four years. In Ben's shoes, I would have made a move sooner."

"But timing is everything." Leo tightened his grip on her hand.

She looked over at him. "Or nothing."

"How so?"

"You make a decision, it turns out great, and then you congratulate yourself on good timing."

"I so agree with you, girlfriend," Eva said. "We get all puffed up about good timing when it's mostly dumb luck. Cleo Marie is a perfect example."

Nick pulled into the hospital's visitor parking lot. "CJ and Isabel don't think so. CJ says this baby timed it perfectly so she'd bring them together."

Eva snorted. "From inside the womb, CJ? Do you believe that?"

"Yes, ma'am." He pulled into a spot next to Jake's truck and shut off the engine. "Just like I believe the bachelor auction was perfect timing for us to find each other."

Fiona couldn't say the same about the auction. Or Operation Santa. When it came to Leo, the timing might never be right.

27

No surprise, the interior of Apple Grove General was well lit. Leo tightened his grip on Fiona's hand as he walked into the reception area. He'd only been in here a couple of times—a broken arm courtesy of an untrained horse and a broken toe compliments of a clumsy one.

A twinkling tree stood in a corner of the lobby and large snowflakes dangled from the ceiling. A tabletop tree sat on the reception counter along with a plate of individually wrapped Christmas cookies.

The receptionist looked familiar and Eva clearly knew her well. A salon client, most likely, and he'd probably met her at Tres Beau, himself. She insisted they all take a cookie before she escorted them personally back to the maternity ward.

Along the way, she glanced at his suit. "Ben must have asked you to play Santa tonight at the Moose."

"Um, not exactly."

"Isn't that his outfit? I was there one Christmas Eve and that looks exactly like—"

"It's Ben's suit, but I—"

"He wore it for me," Fiona's voice was stripped of emotion.

Damn, she'd frozen up.

"Oh, my goodness, what a cute idea! Like that Keith Urban song, *I'll Be Your Santa Tonight.* What a romantic idea."

"Yep." She avoided looking at him.

"There you guys are!" Ben came out of the double doors ahead of them. He looked relieved. "Now everybody's accounted for."

Nick hurried forward, his arm around Eva's shoulders. "Any word?"

"The contractions are closer together, but Cleo's not here yet."

Leo blew out a breath. "Good. I mean, not good that Isabel's still in labor, but I didn't want to miss—"

"I understand, son." Holding the door, he ushered all four of them through it. "Nice suit."

Leo turned back to him. "I'm going to take it to the cleaners, which is why I still have it. I hope it's okay that I—"

"Absolutely." Ben's gaze went to Fiona. "He does the suit proud, don't you think?"

"Sure does."

"Hey, Santa!" Jake sauntered over, a cup of coffee in one hand and a Christmas cookie in the other. "Whatcha gonna bring me this year? I've been a *really* good boy."

"Don't believe a word of it." Millie came up beside him. "If you want an accurate accounting, talk to me."

Leo nodded. "Don't worry. I—"

"Santa!" Henri gestured to one of the couches. "Have a seat, please."

"Why?"

"So I can sit on your knee, of course. I have a very long list. We need to get started."

"Go on." Eva gave him a nudge. "I've got this."

He turned to Fiona. "Do you want me to—"

"Go." Her quick glance pleaded with him. "P-please. It's a good... just go."

Releasing her hand, he crossed to one of the couches and took a seat.

Henri gave him a big smile and perched on his knee. "I want world peace and a pony."

He returned her smile. "I don't suppose the pony is for a certain someone who's making her way into the world tonight."

"Good guess. I want her to have a pony and a peaceful world to ride in. Is that too much to ask?"

"No, ma'am. I'll see to it. Is that all? You said you had a long list."

"I lied." She lowered her voice. "I wanted a chance to explain this nonsense. We came up with it so Fiona could have a little space while we wait for Cleo Marie."

"I figured." He checked on Fi. She was over by the coffee machine with Beth and Eva. "Might work."

"Let's hope so. I'm pulling for you." Giving his shoulder a squeeze, she stood and made way for Lucy.

"I'm next for Santa," Matt announced as Lucy sat down. "The line forms here."

"Your beard's crooked." Lucy adjusted it for him. "What do you think of our plan?"

"It has promise."

"Are you roasting in that suit?"

"It's warm. Not quite as bad as it was at the Moose when we were packed in tight."

"I don't think we factored the warmth of your suit into the plan. You should probably take it off after you finish this gig."

"Thanks for the thought. I'll see how things go." A quick glance confirmed that Fi was still over by the coffee machine with Beth and Eva, her back to him. He faced Lucy. "Now, then, what do you want Santa to bring you, little girl?"

She leaned in and murmured in his ear.

He laughed. "You'll have to talk to Matt. Not my department."

"It would be more fun if you tell him."

"That's a fact. I'll be honored to do it."

"Yay." She stood and motioned to her husband. "Your turn."

Matt settled on his knee and grinned. "What's my wife cooking up now?"

Leo kept his voice down. "She wants a baby."

He gasped and his eyes widened. "She *does?*" He looked over at Lucy standing a few feet away. "You do?"

She nodded.

He leaped up, took two strides and pulled her into his arms. "Awesome."

"Hey, Matt." Leo wasn't sure the guy would hear him, considering how absorbed he was in his wife. "You didn't tell me what you want for Christmas."

"Don't need to, bro." Matt kept his gaze locked with Lucy's. "I just got it."

"My turn, Santa." Kate plopped down on his knee.

He smiled. "And what do you want, Katie-girl?"

"Not a single thing. I have Rafe, a great job, the Buckskin gang and my sister's schooling paid for."

"Good to hear. Then why are you sitting on my knee?"

She leaned closer. "Because that's the plan and I wanted to wish you luck."

His chest tightened. "Thanks, Kate."

"You're welcome." She gave him a quick kiss on the cheek and left as the line continued to grow.

Fiona and her two friends hadn't joined in, which made sense. But Jake and Millie stood to the side and that made no sense at all. Unless Jake had something up his sleeve.

Rafe sauntered up next. "Hey, Santa."

"Hang on a minute, bro. Do you know why Jake and Millie aren't in line?"

"Since it's Jake, no telling."

"I'll try to smoke him out." He glanced in their direction and raised his voice. "Don't you two want to sit on Santa's knee?"

"Oh, I'm doing it," Jake said, "but I'm waiting so I can be at the end and, you know, create the cymbal crash moment."

Leo rolled his eyes. "You do understand that moment belongs to Cleo Marie tonight."

"Who says there can only be one? It's Christmas Eve, in case you didn't notice."

"I noticed. What about you, Millie? Are you gonna sit on Santa's lap?"

"After Jake shows me how it's done."

"So I wouldn't be last." Jake rubbed his chin and nodded. "I guess that works."

"Okay, that's settled. My turn." Rafe perched on Leo's knee. "Did Kate tell you what she wants?"

"Not a single thing. She said she's got it all."

"Yeah?" Happiness gleamed in his eyes. "Then I guess I'll just keep doing what I'm doing."

"Exactly."

After Rafe, the procession moved at a pretty good clip. Would Eva and Beth join in eventually? Likely not if they'd decided Fi needed the support. Jake took his place at the end and Millie followed.

No sign of movement from the three at the coffee machine. Oh, wait. Here they came. Beth got behind Millie and then Eva stepped into line. Fiona took the last spot.

Although she still wasn't looking at him, she'd decided to join in and sit on his knee. That was huge. Millie turned around to chat with them as the line dwindled.

At last it was Jake's turn. "If it isn't little Jacob Lassiter." Leo was ready for some comic relief. "The boy at the top of my naughty list."

"Oh, yeah, oh, yeah." Jake bobbed his head and danced to an imaginary tune with his forefinger raised in triumph. "I'm number one, *numero uno*, top of the heap, cream of the crop—"

"Hey, folks are waiting. Are you going to sit on Santa's knee or not?"

Jake stopped dancing. "Comin' atcha, sleigh boy." He launched himself into Leo's lap.

Damn, the guy was heavy. Good thing he'd sucked in a breath and braced himself.

As he dragged in air, Jake gave him a bear hug and a tender glance. "Hi, Santa."

Leo ducked his head, trying to hide his laughter as his body shook.

"Gotcha, Santa baby. Now listen up. This is what I want for Christmas."

Leo cleared his throat, looked at a grinning Jake and cracked up again. "Back off, man."

Instead, Jake grabbed his ears, tugged him closer and spoke in a stage whisper. "*I want Millie to propose.*"

Millie's gasp was echoed by everyone in the room. Talk about a cymbal crash.

Jake let go of Leo's ears and continued in a conversational tone. "The thing is, Santa, Millie needs to be the one to do it, because only she knows if I'm ready to be her husband. She's right back there." He pointed in her direction. "The one with the red face."

Leo swallowed another burst of laughter. "Do you think this stunt will convince her you're ready?"

"Why not?"

"Because you're acting like a moron."

"She gets a kick out of it when I act like a moron. She pretends she doesn't, but then she eggs me on. She thinks I'm adorable."

Leo snorted. "Do you think he's adorable, Millie?"

"God help me, I do." She walked to the couch. "Move over, Jake. I need Santa's other knee."

"Whatever you say, my love." He put his booted feet on the floor and straightened.

Millie perched on Leo's knee facing Jake. "Give me your hand."

He put his hand out, his gaze laser-focused on Millie's face.

She took a deep breath. "Jake, will you marry me?"

He sandwiched her hand between both of his. "Yes, I will. I love you, Millie. And I'll keep loving you for the rest of my life."

"And I'll love you right back, you crazy cowboy."

The room erupted and Henri threw her hands in the air. "Finally!" After the commotion died down, she spoke again. "When's the wedding, guys?"

Millie turned to her. "Since everyone here is a pro at putting one together in no time, how about next week?"

Henri beamed. "Done."

Leo glanced at Fiona and caught her wiping her eyes. No telling if they were tears of laughter or tears of happiness for Jake and Millie.

Either way, she'd been touched by the unconventional proposal. Much more of these antics and she'd probably fall in love with the Buckskin gang. Would that include him?

_**28**_

What an emotional rollercoaster. Fiona didn't know Jake and Millie well, but who wouldn't laugh at Jake's antics and shed happy tears when Millie proposed? Tonight had given her so much insight into the Buckskin gang. No wonder Eva loved being a part of it.

Eva was convinced she could be, too, but her confidence ebbed as she waited for her two friends to take their turns with Santa. She'd gained plenty of insight into Leo tonight and that had only made the challenge greater.

He'd been tossed into the role by his loving family and he'd handled the assignment with charm and good humor. Clearly they all adored him and he returned the sentiment.

The guy had it all—looks, a great personality and a talent for making wonderful love. Damned intimidating to be pursued by a man with that level of cool going on. But Eva and Beth had coaxed her to face her fears and give the relationship a chance.

Eva stood, flashed her a smile and a subtle thumbs-up before going over to join Nick, Beth and Jared.

A quick scan of the room revealed a group of people working very hard not to look in her direction. She appreciated that effort more than they knew.

Squaring her shoulders and walking toward Leo, she met his gaze. Her brain stalled at the beauty of those blue eyes. What comment had she prepared for her opening gambit? Oh, yeah. "The Buckskin gang is incredible."

"I agree." He held out his hand. "Care to sit?"

"Yes." Breaking eye contact, she took his hand and settled on his knee.

"Your hands are like ice."

"I know." She glanced at him again. "I'm nervous."

His expression warmed. "But you're here. That's progress."

"We'll see." She swallowed. "Beth and Eva think I can do this."

"Do what?"

"Function normally after you take off the suit and beard."

"I don't have to. It's not as uncomfortable as it was at the Moose."

"But you're only doing it to humor me."

"I don't mind."

"I do. I don't want you to be uncomfortable because of me." She stood. "I want you to take it off."

"All right." Leaning over, he pulled off his boots and set them aside. Then he got to his feet and unbuckled the wide black belt.

"What's this?" Nick walked over. "A Santa striptease?"

This would be the perfect time to make a clever, sassy remark. She couldn't come up with one.

Leo responded, though. "Just getting out of the suit, bro. It's one layer too many."

Nick gazed at him. "Just the suit?"

"Nope. The whole ensemble." He took off the jacket and the pants, folding both and laying them on the couch. Next came the hat.

Santa was vanishing quickly, replaced by a swoon-worthy cowboy who was short-circuiting her brain.

"I see." Nick turned to her. "You okay with this?"

"Yep." If by okay he meant ready to pass out from lack of oxygen. When Leo reached for the beard, she focused entirely on Nick. "Perfectly okay." She had to be. It was the only way to show Leo how much she cared about him. To prove she wasn't a coward.

Sweat trickled down her spine. She counted to ten, took a deep breath and faced the man of her dreams.

He ran his fingers through his hair and gave her a lopsided smile. "What do you think?"

Her heart stuttered. Warm blue eyes gazed into hers. A hint of a dimple creased his cheek and his strong jaw had a hint of scruff. She opened her mouth, but nothing came out. She gulped. No, this wasn't happening! *Say something, Fiona!*

"She's here!" CJ burst through the double doors leading to the delivery room, his face shiny with tears. "Cleo Marie is here!'

Leo whooped with joy and rushed toward CJ. On the way, he collided with his brothers as they all raced to mob the new daddy. Before any of them could get to him, he ducked back through the double doors.

"Sorry!" he called over his shoulder. "Gotta go!"

Deprived of CJ, Leo grabbed the nearest person, who happened to be Garrett, and pounded him on the back. Then he turned, his handsome face filled with joy as he hurried in her direction.

His beauty in that moment stunned her more than all the others put together.

Grabbing her around the waist, he lifted her off her feet and swung her around. "She's here! Cleo Marie made it!"

She smiled big and nodded. Because she couldn't get a single word past her throat.

"I'm so happy I don't know what to do with myself." He gave her a squeeze and set her back on her feet. Then he took her hand. "Let's go find Henri. God, this is wonderful. CJ's a dad! And I'm an uncle!"

"Here you go, Uncle Leo!" Jake handed him a pink bubblegum cigar. "Want one, Fiona? Sure you do. The band has Cleo Marie's name on it." He thrust one into her hand, gave Leo a hug and left to pass out more cigars.

"What a guy." Leo glanced at the band. "Ordering personalized ones." He tucked it in his shirt pocket. "There's Henri." He wrapped an arm around Fiona's shoulders and gave her a sideways hug before they started over to the corner where

Henri stood with the Babes. "I'm so glad you're here, Fi."

"Uh-huh." That was all she had. The only response. But no one noticed besides her. For now, she had a pass. The spotlight was elsewhere.

Henri reached out for him. "Hey, Leo." She gave him a tight hug. "Pretty great, huh?"

"Sure is. Will we get to see her?"

"I think so." Henri alternated between laughing and wiping tears from her eyes with Ben's bandana. "Maybe. Ben went to ask one of the nurses. We're a little short on info about how maternity wards operate these days. Fiona, do you know the protocol?"

Fiona cleared her throat. Didn't help. "Uh-uh."

"Personalized cigars!" Jake approached with a fistful.

Henri held out her hand. "I'll take one for me and one for Ben."

"You've got it. Who wants one? Ed, I'm sure you do."

"You know it." Ed ran it under her nose. "Not quite Havana quality, but it'll do." She winked at Jake. "Well done."

"I want one." Josette held out her hand.

Red took six and started distributing them. "Peggy, you and your hubby each need one. Pam, one for you and one for your fire chief back at the station. Lucy, here you go. We'll have a bubble-blowing contest while we wait to find out whether we get to see Cleo Marie."

Leo glanced at Jake. "Did you just happen to have these with you tonight?"

"I had a hunch so I put them in the truck before we left for the Moose. There's more in that duffle over by the coffeepot. Isabel will want some for her family when they finally get here." He lowered his voice. "Thanks for the help with my Christmas wish, Santa."

"Anytime, bro. Quick thinking."

"Didn't know if it would work. Thank God it did." Jake turned to Fiona. "I admit we're a crazy bunch, but usually we try to space out these major events. A proposal and a baby on the same night is not the norm. Hope you're not too discombobulated."

"Nope." What a whopper. Her brain had turned to mush, and it got worse every time she looked at Leo. He was a god. She couldn't reconcile his face with the man who'd turned her inside out in the dark.

"I think it's great that you talked this guy into taking off the whiskers. I guess that means you'll be coming to the Christmas dinner. You'll love the video. It's always a—"

"We get to see her!" Ben's voice boomed out as he crossed the room toward Henri. "Just for a little while. No holding or kissing yet. CJ's bringing Isabel out in a wheelchair and she'll be holding Cleo Marie. You can gather around the doorway, but not too close."

Henri let out a happy sigh. "That's good enough for now. I just want to lay eyes on that little cherub. I can wait on the holding and squeezing part."

"Same here." Leo smiled at Fiona. "Let's go meet Cleo Marie."

She stood by his side as Ed arranged them in a semi-circle in front of the double doors. "If you have gum, take it out." Ed gave them all the eagle-eye. "I don't want anybody popping a bubble and scaring that baby. And besides, you'll look dumb on the video."

"Hang on. I'm not leaving this to chance." Pam grabbed a paper napkin near the plate of cookies and started at the far end. "Give me those wads of gum."

Peggy laughed. "Once a den mother, always a den mother."

Leo grinned at Fiona. "Better cough it up if you have some. Don't just stick it under your tongue. Pam has X-ray vision."

She held up her wrapped cigar.

"Alrighty, then." He peered at her. "You doing okay, Fi?"

Caught in the intensity of his gaze, she almost swallowed her tongue. "Um..."

A nurse propped open the double doors and stepped back.

Leo clutched her hand tighter as a wheelchair rolled out of a room down the hall and turned. CJ gripped the handles and started forward, his mile-wide smile lighting up the entire corridor.

Isabel looked tired but happy. She kept peering at the wrapped bundle in her arms.

CJ pushed the wheelchair as far as the open doors. "Here we are." His voice was husky as he looked down at his little family. "Izzy, can you hold her up a little so they can see her face?"

"Sure." Cradling Cleo Marie in her arms, she rearranged the blanket and turned her toward her fans. The little girl's eyes were closed and one impossibly small fist protruded out of the blanket. A bit of blond hair covered the top of her head like peach fuzz.

Leo's breath caught and he moved closer to Fiona. "Isn't she amazing?"

"Mm."

CJ leaned over Isabel's shoulder, reached down and stroked a finger over his daughter's cheek. Then he looked up, his emotion-filled gaze circling the group. "You can't imagine what it means that you all..." He paused, too overcome to continue. Then he drew in a breath. "Thank you for being here for us."

Henri sniffed. "She's beautiful, CJ. You're all beautiful, all three of you."

"Thank you, Henri." Isabel smiled. "Thanks, gang." Then she murmured something to CJ and he nodded.

"I need to take my ladies back to the room so they can rest." His glance swept the group one more time. "Merry Christmas."

The nurse closed the doors, followed by a collective sigh.

"Best Christmas present ever," Henri said, her voice unsteady. "Let's head home, everybody. We have a lot to celebrate tomorrow."

29

Nick caught Leo's eye. "Ready?"

Leo glanced at Fiona.

She nodded, holding up a finger and pointing. "Coat."

Uh-oh. Something was off. He'd had a hunch earlier, and she'd avoided his gaze just now as she went to fetch her coat. He remained uneasy on the trip back to town.

He, Nick and Eva had plenty to talk about. Cleo Marie's arrival dominated the conversation, although Jake and Millie's surprise decision to get married was discussed, too. Fiona barely said two words.

Maybe her newcomer status was part of the issue. But the Fiona he'd made love to in the dark wouldn't have let that stop her. She knew all the players even if she hadn't been around that long. She should have dived right in with enthusiasm.

"If you could drop us beside my truck in the rear parking lot of the Moose, that would be the most helpful," he said as they approached the town limits. "I'll drive Fiona over to her place."

"Got it." Nick pulled into the alley that led to the rear parking lot and glanced at his dashboard clock. "Hey, it's after midnight. Merry Christmas, you two." He left the truck running as he hopped out and put down his seat to let them out.

"A very Merry Christmas." Eva swiveled in her seat. "We'll see you both tomorrow, right?"

"Right." Leo grabbed the Santa suit and helped Fiona out. "Thanks again for the ride, bro."

"Yes, thank you," Fiona echoed.

As Nick pulled away, Leo handed her into the passenger seat of his truck. "Sorry it's so cold."

"I'm fine. You're..." She gestured at his shirtsleeves, her gaze on his chest.

"Like I said, I run hot." Not hot enough to keep from shivering, but he was sick of putting on the Santa jacket. He hurried around to the driver's side, climbed in and started the engine. Before buckling his seatbelt, he put the Santa suit in the backseat and managed to wiggle into his very cold jacket.

Then he buckled up, put the truck in gear and pulled out of the parking lot. "The Moose is still going strong."

"I'm not—"

"I'm not suggesting we go in." But he longed to recapture the mood they'd created when they were dancing.

Cleo Marie's birth had been awesome and Jake's engagement to Millie was a bonus. They'd be married before New Year's Eve. Or maybe on New Year's Eve. A cymbal crash, as Jake would say.

Several of his brothers were over the moon tonight—CJ was a new dad, Jake was engaged to Millie at long last, and Matt and Lucy could start working on that baby they wanted. Good news. But no point in denying it, his budding relationship with Fiona had taken a hit.

He lobbed a conversational softball. "Crazy night, huh?"

"Yeah."

"Like Jake said, we usually don't double up on the life-changing events. This was unusual."

"Uh-huh."

He pulled up in front of her shop. "Just so you know, you don't have to make that dinner tomorrow."

"I know."

"Unless you want to." He reached for the ignition.

Her hand darted out, stopping him. "Don't."

Dread pooled in the pit of his stomach. "You want to take a spin around the square?"

"No." She turned to him, staring at a point over his shoulder. "I was hoping... Eva and Beth said..."

She was struggling to finish a sentence. Not a good sign. "You did great tonight. I know it was a lot, but we just have to—"

"No."

"No?"

"I can't... do this."

"Do what?"

"Talk. To you."

"Fi—"

"No, Leo. Just... no." She pulled her hand away and unfastened her seat belt.

He opened his door and the dome light flicked on. "Let me come in. We can discuss this. Work it out."

She paused, her breath hitching as she met his gaze. "No."

Panic set in. "This isn't over. *We're* not over."

Her gaze skittered away. "Yes, we are." She reached for the door handle.

"Wait! You have to know I'm in—"

"*No!*" Her voice was filled with anguish. She scrambled out, flung the door closed and ran across the ice-crusted sidewalk.

"Fi!" He leaped out. She'd fall for sure.

But she didn't. She was inside in no time.

He had a key. But using it would be futile. She didn't want him there.

30

Sleep was not Fiona's friend, not even when she abandoned her memory-laden bedroom and settled on her couch. She finally gave up, dressed in her most comfortable sweat suit and made coffee. Once the coffee finished brewing, she ate a balanced breakfast—a Christmas cookie in each hand.

Ending a hot affair on Christmas Eve sucked, but it had one thing going for it. She had a full day alone to gather her forces. Her two best friends were with their sweethearts so she wouldn't have to put on a brave face for them. The shop was closed, so she wouldn't have to force herself to smile at customers, either.

On the flip side, she'd have to fill the day with something or she'd go bonkers. She sorted through the options. She was too restless to read or watch movies. Aha, she could go jogging! And pull a hamstring. She'd never jogged a day in her life.

A long ramble through the countryside? Nope. Without a major distraction, she'd spend it reliving the past four days. And nights. Cleaning her apartment had the same drawback without the change of scenery.

She meandered downstairs and turned on the shop lights. Hey! She'd scheduled the store's inventory for January, but she was the boss. It was almost January. She could start today.

The process would engage her brain and help her block unproductive thoughts about a certain cowboy. And how his blue eyes had warmed when he'd pulled her close on the dance floor. And how she'd melted down at the hospital and in his truck....

Groaning, she marched upstairs, refilled her coffee mug and grabbed the rest of the cookies. Inventory. Her saving grace.

Hours later she congratulated herself on her choice. She was damn close to finishing the job. She'd finished the cookies, too, requiring her to switch to a different food group—an elegant box of dark chocolates from one of her customers.

Eating sweets all day had given her a sugar high, but better high than low, right? At least she'd switched to decaf when she'd started shaking so much she was dropping things.

As the light coming through the front windows began to fade, she debated whether to go upstairs and fix some real food for supper.

Supper. It was almost dusk! How could she have forgotten?

Ten minutes later, armed with a thermos of hot chocolate, a package of pretzels and Winifred's journal, she drove her five-year-old red Honda hybrid over to the Apple Grove cemetery. She'd bought a red car because it was her favorite color, but it wasn't the best choice for a covert stakeout.

Couldn't be helped. Beth and Eva both had ginormous trucks which would stand out even more, especially Beth's with the Racy Lace logo on both doors. Not many people knew she had a car because she kept it in a covered space behind her building and seldom used it.

Everything she needed was within walking distance, including the cemetery. Except she'd last about five minutes standing out in the cold waiting to see if anybody left a holiday wreath on Winifred's grave.

Fortunately, Winifred was buried in her family's plot near the front entrance. The Bartons had secured it more than a hundred years ago, so they'd scored a premier location.

The parking area to the left of the entrance was empty. No surprise, there. She could have parked right across from the gravesite, but she wanted to leave that for Winifred's secret lover. Instead she chose a spot four spaces over.

She could see fine. Dusk had fallen, and Winifred's white marble headstone gleamed in the light from the lampposts on either side of the tall, wrought iron double gate that stood permanently open. No wreath yet on Winifred's grave.

The two similar stones on either side of Winifred looked like many of the ones in the cemetery, weathered and crusted with lichen. Trees had grown behind the plot, two stately pines on either side of an oak, leafless now.

Because she knew the story of Winifred's soldier fiancé dying just days before the wedding, the placement of the stones made sense. Witnessing her grief, her parents had concluded she'd never marry. They'd chosen to give her the middle plot and they'd taken one on either side, surrounding her with their love.

Leaving the motor running, Fiona turned off the headlights and opened her thermos of hot chocolate. Her phone pinged.

Eva. *Are you there?*

Yep. Nothing yet.

Eva had remembered. By now she'd be at the Buckskin and would have heard the latest. She probably wouldn't bring up that subject in a text conversation, though.

Then Beth texted. *Any news?*

Waiting. After texting that to Beth, she set up a group text for when she had something to report.

Maybe nothing would happen, but she'd read Winifred's journal, the words and the emotions that hadn't been put into words. Winifred had loved that man and he'd loved her back. Who else would sneak over here on Christmas and put a wreath on her grave?

She pulled a pretzel out of the sack and munched on it as she sipped her hot chocolate. The snack kept the caper from turning into a scene from *A Christmas Carol.* She had no interest in meeting any ghosts tonight.

Her phone pinged, then pinged again. Identical texts. *Anything?*

She answered them on the group text she'd created. *Still waiting. I promise I'll text you if anything happens.*

No sooner had she sent it than headlights appeared in her rearview mirror. She shut off the engine and put her hot chocolate in the cup holder. Maybe he, and she had to believe it was a man, hadn't seen the clouds of condensation coming out of her tailpipe.

But her presence would be noticed. Chances were good he'd deposit the wreath and leave, not wanting to make contact with whoever was here. She slid down in the seat so the car would look unoccupied.

Whoever he was drove a truck. It rumbled closer and parked in the exact space she'd left for him. Her view was limited because she'd hunkered down so low, but the top part of the truck was visible. It didn't shine in the lamppost light. Its paint job had faded and it had a dent in the back fender.

The driver's door opened. Her pulse hammered as the driver climbed down with slow, measured movements. Didn't look like a woman, but she shouldn't jump to conclusions just because she so desperately wanted it to be a man.

Whoever it was walked around to the passenger side. Was someone else in there? That would blow her entire theory. But no, the driver closed the passenger door and walked toward the open gate carrying... something.

When he stepped into the light, she clapped a hand over her mouth so she wouldn't let out a whoop. He was holding a wreath.

Grabbing her phone, she sent a text to Eva and Beth. *He's here. Just took a wreath into the cemetery!*

Eva responded first. *Do you recognize him? What's he driving?*

An old truck, faded paint.

Could be anybody. Try to get a better look at him. Tall? Short?

On the tall side. Looks slim. Older. Have to believe it's a guy.

Beth chimed in. *I'll ask Jared who drives an old truck around here.*

Thanks. Fiona scooted up enough so that she could see over the dash. The person went straight to Winifred's grave, leaned the wreath against the headstone, and dropped to one knee.

Fiona's breath caught. That simple act of devotion brought tears to her eyes. That was a guy. No question about it.

Several seconds passed. The man struggled to his feet—another clue, and walked slowly out of the cemetery, shoulders slumped.

Her heart ached for him. She'd had some wild idea she'd be able to ID him, but not in this dim light. To do that, she'd have to get out of her car and confront him. That would be so wrong.

He approached his truck and walked to the driver's side. Then he turned to face her car. He stood there for several seconds. Then he started in her direction.

Her phone was going crazy with texts from Beth and Eva. She silenced it and repositioned herself in the seat. The man rounded the hood of her car and tapped on her driver's side window.

She rolled it down and gazed up at Orville Dubois. She'd been right.

"You're the lady from the paper store."

"Yes."

"Why are you here?"

"I have something that belongs to you. From Winifred."

He frowned. "I can't imagine—"

"Will you come sit with me?" She pushed the button to unlock the passenger door.

He smiled, revealing a trace of the dashing man who'd captured Winifred's heart. "I'd be a fool to refuse an invitation from a beautiful lady."

As he walked around to the passenger side, she tucked the thermos and bag of pretzels behind her seat. She laid the journal in her lap.

He climbed in, bringing with him the scent of a spicy cologne.

"You smell nice."

"It was her favorite cologne."

"You loved her very much." She didn't look at him. Gazing out the windshield seemed more respectful.

"More than you can imagine. She was my heart, my soul, but she rejected me."

Fiona made an educated guess. "On Christmas Day?"

"On Christmas Day. I asked her to marry me. I wanted to be with her for the rest of my life. I wanted to go to sleep in her arms and wake up to her smile. She said it would never work. We were creatures of the night. That's all we'd ever be."

That was a sucker punch to her gut. "You ended it?"

"She did. I would have gone on forever, accepting whatever crumbs she would give me, but she said that wasn't fair. I should find a woman who'd be the partner I needed."

"Because she loved you."

"But I didn't want anyone else. Several times I tried to reconnect with her, but she wouldn't see me."

"That's so sad."

"It's very sad. But I thought it was very private, too. Evidently not."

"It's still sort of private. My friend Eva bought Winifred's house."

"I know that."

"She found this in a box in the attic."

"A journal?"

"About your love affair."

He sucked in a breath. "You've read it?"

"Yes. And full disclosure, so have Eva and my friend Beth. But that's it. Only three of us."

"And now you're giving it to me."

"That was my idea, if I could figure out who you were. She didn't identify you in the journal."

He took a deep breath. "Because I was never real to her. I was a fantasy. And I wanted to be her partner."

"But if you read this, you'll know how much she cared. She truly loved you."

"In her way." A trace of bitterness tinged his words. "But we could have had so much more."

This was hitting way too close to home. "Maybe she gave you all she could."

"I believe she did, at the time, but if she'd screwed up her courage... we could have had it all."

31

The aroma of beef stew filled the air in the two-story ranch house that Leo had grown to love almost as much as the bunkhouse. Henri had never been a fan of turkey, and he'd been relieved to discover she regularly served beef stew on Christmas. His memories of his family's traditional Christmas dinners weren't great, so any deviation was welcome.

Over the years, one pot had grown to two. This time Henri had made it early so they could take some to CJ and Isabel in the middle of the day. Because Isabel's parents and sister continued to have travel issues, a visit from the Buckskin gang bringing servings of beef stew and pumpkin pie had been a big hit.

Another glimpse of Cleo Marie had provided conversation for the rest of the afternoon. Following tradition, everyone rotated between working in the kitchen and playing board games in Henri's living room. A debate about the baby's light wisps of hair hadn't ended yet. Was it newborn fuzz or evidence she'd be blond like her daddy?

The little girl had opened her eyes when Jake had been in the room and he'd sworn they were CJ's exact shade of blue. Others claimed a newborn's eyes could change color, just like a newborn's hair.

Leo contributed to both debates, looking up info on his phone and relaying it to the group. Focusing on Cleo Marie helped fill the aching void in his chest. Teasing Jake and Millie about their gonzo proposal scenario and chiming in on their plans for a New Year's Eve wedding helped, too.

He took a moment to tell Henri about Mrs. Warner and little Georgie. Henri promised that she and the Babes would help Georgie's mom find a job that would pay enough to hire a sitter. He was glad he'd mentioned it, but unfortunately the subject had Fiona memories attached. He opened another bottle of cider.

Then Eva disappeared into a back room with her phone. That move wouldn't have to be related to Fiona, but it was dusk and Fi should be heading over to the cemetery about now.

When Eva came back, she had a whispered conversation with Nick. Had to be about Fiona's stakeout at the cemetery. Last night Leo had been curious about the outcome. Now it was just one more thing to let go of. He finished off the cider and went to fetch more.

Ed's video had been downloaded to Ben's laptop. Between dinner and dessert, he'd hook it up to Henri's flat screen so they could all watch. Leo kept eyeing the laptop sitting over by the TV.

It looked perfectly innocent, as if it wasn't armed with a video that would break his heart. His favorite part of a Buckskin Christmas had become his worst nightmare.

When dinner was delayed because Henri forgot to put the rolls in the oven, he was thrilled. Maybe he'd be toasted by the time Ben cued up the video and watching it wouldn't hurt as much.

Eventually the rolls were ready and the line formed to cruise the feast laid out on the dining room table. Filling a plate and then jockeying for a spot in the living room was half the fun. Or it had been, before his dreams imploded.

Nick coached Eva, the newbie, to be bold.

"How bold?" Eva gazed at him.

He winked. "Bold like musical chairs. Which means watch out for Jake. He cheats."

"I don't cheat." Jake puffed out his chest. "I strategize. Right, Millie?"

She smiled. "Let's just say you're a master at walking a fine line."

"I like that. Maybe I'll have it engraved on my tombstone."

"Keep holding up *this* line and you'll be needing that tombstone sooner than you think." Rafe sent him a warning glance.

Leo's appetite had vanished and he didn't care how long Jake took to get his food. But he joined in the razzing as the Brotherhood gave Jake a hard time for being a slowpoke. He was determined to keep up appearances.

It was likely a wasted effort. Everyone in the room had the relevant news about Fiona. But he didn't want to shine a light on his personal misery tonight. It was Christmas. He'd deal.

He chose the end of the line, though, because it reduced the likelihood that anyone would notice he didn't dish himself much. Garrett was ahead of him and had just filled his plate and stew bowl when somebody knocked on the door.

Leo took a breath to calm his jangling nerves. It wasn't her. Couldn't be her. Not after what she'd said to him last night. Or more to the point, hadn't been able to say.

"I'll get it." Garrett put down his food at the end of the table.

Smiling to himself, Leo picked up a stew bowl and plate. Before the initiation, Garrett would never have presumed to answer Henri's door. But now he was a member of the Brotherhood, a man who subscribed to the Brotherhood's creed. *What would Charley do?* He'd answer the door.

If Leo had to guess, he'd say one of the Babes had dropped by. But the woman's voice that drifted from the open door wasn't one of the Babes.

His mouth went dry. He was hallucinating. Wishful thinking. Shouldn't have had the third bottle of cider.

As Garrett brought the visitor into the living room, Leo put down his half-filled plate and walked through the archway.

"I found this Christmas elf on the doorstep." Garrett managed to sound casual about it. "She wants to sing for us."

He couldn't breathe. Clearly the elf costume was significant, but he couldn't figure out why.

She glanced his way, her cheeks flushed. Clearly this wasn't easy for her.

Then she faced the group in the living room. The men had scrambled to their feet at her arrival. "Sorry I'm late. Henri, this is for you. Hostess gift." She held out a leather journal.

Henri walked over and took it, giving Fiona a warm smile. "That's fabulous. Thank you."

"So, here's my song, inspired by... family. And love." Taking a deep breath, she launched into *We Wish You a Merry Christmas* except she substituted *I* for *we* and added a jaunty dance step to the number.

Her bravery and fortitude cracked his heart wide open as she pushed her way through the words of the song. She was battling her demons so they'd have a chance. If he'd loved her before, it was nothing compared to the fierce emotion that gripped him now.

She finished, bowing as the group cheered. The applause kept going, not because it was a spectacular performance, although it was cute as hell. But everyone in the room understood what her return meant to him.

Blushing, she sent him another sideways glance.

He got the message. She needed a graceful way to leave the stage. He stepped forward and took her arm. She was trembling. "Fiona and I have some business to discuss. If you'll excuse us, we're heading out to the porch."

"Turn off the porch light on your way out!" Jake called after them.

He didn't. He wanted to see her, wanted to look into her eyes as she said whatever she'd come to say.

She'd left her red wool coat on the coat tree by the door. He helped her into it before putting on his jacket. Then he ushered her out to the porch.

After he closed the door, he hauled her into his arms. "You're here."

"I needed to—"

He cut her off with a kiss. She didn't need to tell him anything. If she'd come to this dinner, the future was bright. Starting now.

She kissed him back, but then she pulled away. "Don't you want to know why I'm here?"

"Don't care." He lowered his head.

She dodged away. "Well, I care and I want you to hear me out."

He paused, intrigued by her bold response. She was speaking in complete sentences again. He didn't want to stop that momentum, especially while she was looking right at him. "Yes, ma'am."

"I went to the cemetery tonight."

"I thought so. Figured that's who Eva was texting with."

"I was in communication with her and Beth, but they don't know how it turned out. You're the first person I've told. For a reason."

He gazed at her in breathless anticipation. "What reason?"

"I don't want to be like Winifred Barton. I want to be like Henri Fox."

"Meaning?"

"Forty-some years ago, Winifred was madly in love with Orville Dubois and—"

"The old guy who sits by the potbellied stove in the Apple Barrel General Store?"

"Like I said, that was more than forty years ago. He was several years younger than she was, and although he didn't see it as a problem, she did. She broke off their secret affair because he wanted to marry her. She said they were creatures of the night and could never be more."

He tightened his hold. "Sounds like someone I know."

"That's why I'm here. She broke his heart. I don't want to break yours. Or mine."

Warmth filled his chest. "That's very good news."

"Henri was scared last night, but she sang anyway. For Ben's sake, but for hers, too. I was petrified in there, but—"

"You didn't look scared." It was only a tiny fib.

"Oh, I'm sure I did, but when I finished, I felt like a million bucks."

"I'm so in love with you, Fi." He couldn't go another second without saying it.

Her gaze locked with his. "I was worried that you're only in love with the seductive person you met in the dark."

"I know. But I'm not. I spent quality time with the person wearing the elf suit."

"That's exactly why I wore it. My goal is to blend those two versions of me so you have the whole picture."

"That should take about five minutes."

She grinned. "Tonight?"

"It's a date." He dragged in a breath. "And let me clarify. I'm not just *in* love with you. I love you. Full stop."

She looked up at him as the light in her eyes grew brighter. And brighter still. "I'm finally ready to believe that."

"Thank God."

"You had me from the moment you did your trick-riding at the auction. But I wouldn't let myself love you."

"And now?"

"I'm going to love you with everything in me. I'm going to love you like you've never been loved. I'm going to—"

He kissed her, making that magic connection. She loved him. *She loved him.* Did that mean.... He lifted his head. "No more darkness?"

"No more darkness. Only light. And love."

"One more kiss. Then we'll go inside." As his lips met hers, he made a silent promise. He would give her all the light and love in his heart. Because that was what Charley would do.

* * * * *

Newest member of the Brotherhood, Garret
Whittaker, proves there's more to him than
meets the eye in STAND-UP COWBOY, book
seven in the Buckskin Brotherhood series!

* * * * *

New York Times bestselling author Vicki Lewis Thompson's love affair with cowboys started with the Lone Ranger, continued through Maverick, and took a turn south of the border with Zorro. She views cowboys as the Western version of knights in shining armor, rugged men who value honor, honesty and hard work. Fortunately for her, she lives in the Arizona desert, where broad-shouldered, lean-hipped cowboys abound. Blessed with such an abundance of inspiration, she only hopes that she can do them justice.

For more information about this prolific author, visit her website and sign up for her newsletter. She loves connecting with readers.

VickiLewisThompson.com